STAR TREK®
nemesis

STAR TREK®
NEMESIS

novelization by
J. M. Dillard

story by
John Logan & Rick Berman
& Brent Spiner

screenplay by
John Logan

Star Trek® **created by Gene Roddenberry**

POCKET BOOKS
New York   London   Toronto   Sydney   Singapore

POCKET BOOKS, a division of Simon & Schuster UK Ltd, Africa House, 64–78 Kingsway, London WC2B 6AH

ISBN: 0-7434-7866-5

First Pocket Books paperback printing August 2003

10 9 8 7 6 5 4 3 2 1

All photography by Sam Emerson, except page 221, by Ron Nomura

Printed and bound in Great Britain by Cox & Wyman Ltd, Reading, Berkshire

For John Logan,
one of the nicest *Star Trek* fans I've ever met

Acknowledgments

Books are never written in a vacuum: there are always people (other than the writer) who help the process in many ways. I always wind up forgetting to thank people who deserve it, but here's my best attempt to mention all of those who were kind to me, who gave me information that made a difference, who cajoled, pampered, and calmed me, and/or were just all-around nice:

First, I have to kneel down and grovel gratefully before John Logan, who wrote the screenplay for *Star Trek Nemesis*. John is more than nice, as I called him the book's dedication: the man is downright adorable, helpful, reverent, and trustworthy. John Logan, so overwhelmed with work and incredibly busy during the final days of the film's shooting, called me and spoke to me for a good half hour about the film and gave me basic information about scenes which had been cut. I've included what I hope is a reasonable version of those scenes here. John also gave me his home phone number—Do you have *any* idea how utterly unusual that is for someone who works in Hollywood?—and told me to call him anytime I had questions. John is a sweetheart. John is a doll. *And* John is a total *Star Trek* fan; this allowed him to give *Nemesis* a wonderful sense of resonance with the *Star Trek: The Next Generation* series. It is, in my not-too-humble opinion, one of the best *Star Trek* films ever written. Any film that John writes, you go see. Understood?

Now that I have made a feeble attempt to give John his due, let me grovel now before Margaret Clark, the editor of this novel. Margaret, you see, is A Very Important Person to me. Why is she so Important? Because she had the graciousness and kindness to give the honor of writing this novelization to me; and besides, I may as well mention her here because she's smart and terrifically funny and a downright pleasure to work for.

I must also thank another incredibly sweet person while I'm on a roll: Michael Okuda. Mike, if you don't know by now, is a veteran of *Star Trek* series (plural) and movies; he is one of the fantastic artists who has made *Star Trek* the visual wonder that it is. Through his nonfiction guides on *Star Trek* and through other means, he has provided great help with the technical aspects that further enriched the book and made it better than it would otherwise be.

Thanks also go to the always helpful, always amiable Paula Block. Her assistance made it possible for me to describe a Reman, the *Argo,* Shinzon, the desert aliens, Troi's famous wedding dress, and a multitude of other creatures, people, places, and things that I simply would not have been able to tell you about otherwise. To her, and to Riki Leigh Arnold and Mary Beth Verhunce, I am eternally in debt.

Now, to all of you whom I've forgotten to thank: Please insert your name here, and consider it done.

Jeanne Dillard

April 2002

Somewhere in southern California

Introduction

by John Logan

Captain Kirk and Me

I first met Captain James T. Kirk in 1966. He was on his original five-year mission, and I was living in New Jersey.

My mother recently reminded me that I would become quite ferocious when she told me *Star Trek* was on too late and I had to go to bed. I would kick and scream and appeal to the heavens about the injustice of it all. Now, you don't know me, but I am not given to kicking and screaming. But something about that show apparently made me a little crazy.

It still does.

When I was growing up we moved every two or three years. My father is a naval architect, and I spent my youth in various port cities all over the country. It was tough and traumatic regularly leaving my friends and making new ones, but I think my passion for *Star Trek* is a direct result of all those moves. No matter where we were living—California or New Jersey or Mississippi—Kirk and the crew of the mighty *Enterprise* were always there; a safe and familiar harbor.

As I grew up I devoured the original series in reruns. While not realizing it at the time, the exciting morality tales Gene Roddenberry created had a profound influence on me. Any notions I currently have of justice, heroism, compassion, and humane behavior probably originated with Captain Kirk and his comrades. Since you are reading this book, you will probably agree with me that *Star Trek* offers important life lessons for those willing to listen. I did and feel I am a better person for it.

I was Captain Kirk for every Halloween I can remember. I built all the *Enterprise* models and staged elaborate battles with my Klingon battle cruisers. I picked the most likely looking G.I. Joes and turned them into Kirk and Spock. I watched the shows and read the novels all the way through college and beyond. Yes, I went through the inevitable ribbing from my friends. They didn't quite get my fascination with Kirk and Spock or Picard and Data. I was a geek, probably harmless but you couldn't be quite sure.

You can imagine, then, my singular joy when I was able to call my mother and tell her that I—her little Captain Kirk—was writing the next *Star Trek* movie. She finally agreed it was probably a good thing that she occasionally looked the other way and let me stay up past my bedtime.

I am a *Trekkie*. Proud of it.

Imagining Nemesis

If you haven't seen the movie, or want to be surprised by the plot turns in J. M. Dillard's wonderful novel, stop reading now!

My friend Brent Spiner first brought me into the world of *Trek*. A mutual pal, Linda Emond, was playing opposite him in the Broadway revival of *1776*. She asked me if I wanted to see the show and then have dinner with Brent. Of course I jumped at the chance to meet Commander Data. It didn't take long for me to realize that Brent is even more interesting, idiosyncratic, and amusing than Data. He is smart, sensitive, and has an almost scary, encyclopedic knowledge of every movie ever made. Not to mention history, literature, politics . . .

It will probably come as no surprise to learn that Brent is also howlingly funny. During the long days on the set of *Nemesis*, he could be guaranteed to have me weeping in laughter with his James Doohan imitation.

We hit it off immediately and it wasn't long before the idea of my writing a *Trek* movie came up. The next time I was in Los Angeles (I live in Illinois), Brent brought me by Paramount to meet the estimable Rick Berman.

So there I was, a lifelong fan about to step into the veritable heart of *Trek*. And to meet the Wizard himself.

Rick Berman, as you may know, is the commander-in-chief of the *Star Trek* empire. Since Gene Roddenberry's death he has created and produced the television shows and the movies. He is in many ways the stepfather of *Trek*. And, believe me, we are lucky to have him. In my many Hollywood adventures, I have rarely come across a producer so involved, so intelligent, and so committed to excellence as Rick. He is a truly compassionate and *decent* man. Every fan who has ever enjoyed a *Next Generation*, *Deep Space Nine*, *Voyager* or *Enterprise* episode—or one of the recent movies—owes a big debt of gratitude to that great teddy bear of a man.

I had thought for weeks about what I was going to say when I met Rick. My mind was swimming with ideas about what makes a great *Trek* movie. The model for me was always *Star Trek II: The Wrath of Khan*, which I think worked on every level. The great Nicholas Meyer (who directed *Khan*) and Jack Sowards (who wrote the screenplay) did something very smart in that movie: they gave Captain Kirk glasses. With that simple act, they acknowledged that fact that these characters were getting older; that time was moving on for them. I felt it was important to capture this sense of continuity with *The Next Generation* crew. Captain Picard and his shipmates are too vibrant and vital to be trapped in a little time bubble called the *Enterprise*, never growing or changing, perpetually going on new missions until the end of time.

Most important, I wanted to write a movie for the fans. For people like me who really know these characters and love watching them grow and face new challenges. My idea was to focus the story very tightly on the *Enterprise* crew. Essentially, write a "bottle show" where we would spend a lot of time on ships and with our featured characters.

My hope was to write a movie about the special *family* that is the *Enterprise* crew; a family that is growing and evolving. I wanted to dramatize our heroes at the moment of change and show Picard dealing with it all. From the very beginning I imagined starting the movie with the wedding of Riker and Deanna and ending it with *Captain* Riker finally leaving the *Enterprise* to assume his own command.

Frankly, I was a little nervous at first about voicing all these somewhat radical ideas to Rick. After all, one of the great rules of a franchise movie is that you must return all the toys to the toy box when you are done. To my delight, Rick loved the idea of trying to do something different. He talked about his desire to see these characters grow and change; of seeing Picard and his friends facing real life challenges.

And, needless to say, we didn't return all the toys to the toy box.

Good-bye to Data

It was Brent who first brought up the idea of killing Data.

I was horrified. It saddened me to even think about it. I adore Data. How could I write his death? I must say I grappled with this emotional issue for a long time. Eventually, Brent and I had a long and serious dinner where we talked about what killing Data would actually mean. I knew it would be devastating to our audience. Should we really do it? Brent spoke movingly about his affection for Data and the fifteen years he had spent with him. But he felt that this story was worth it. In a movie about family, about the choices we make, what more moving or emotional climax could there be then Data sacrificing himself for his friends?

Rick, Brent, and I finally came to feel that if we could give Data a dignified and honorable passing, an ending appropriate to the character, it was worth trying.

In retrospect I think we made the right choice. The B-4 offers some hope that Data's spirit isn't entirely gone and the death of Data and subsequent mourning scenes are, for me, the most powerful in the movie.

Twist and Turns: Developing the Story

Rick, Brent, and I worked closely for about a year. Whenever I was in LA we would gather in Rick's rather unprepossessing office and bat story ideas around wildly. The plot gradually began to unfold. It was a very happy collaboration where all three of us contributed important ideas and elements to the narrative.

As we worked, I was amused to learn that I knew a hell of a lot more *Star Trek* minutiae than either of them! Imagine sitting there with Rick Berman and Brent Spiner and lecturing *them* on Worf's family history or the politics on Romulus! I would frequently interrupt our meetings to say something appropriately geekish like: "No, wait, we can't do that because in Episode 262 we learned that Lore was actually the *fourth* android Dr. Soong created!" On such occasions they would roll their eyes and patiently wait for me to finish. They were very indulgent when my flights of *Trekkie* fandom took wing.

Rick and Brent were great collaborators and fully supported some of my more radical notions. In fact, one of the very first ideas I pitched to Rick was having the *Enterprise* ram the villain's ship, pretty much destroying yet another *Enterprise* in the process. He thought about it for a second and then smiled and said, "That sounds good." Brent became the ultimate "go-to-guy." Whenever I would write or think myself into a corner, I would call Brent and lay the problem before him. A typical exchange:

JOHN

Okay, Brent, I have Picard and Data on the
villain's ship. They need to get off and
they can't use the transporter. And there
are all these Remans chasing them! I don't
know what to do! They're gonna be killed!!
HELP ME!

BRENT

```
Hmm . . . (five second pause) . . . How about
they fly a shuttle through the inside of the
ship and then smash through a window?
```

As a fan, it was thrilling for me to sit there and help chart this part of the continuing *Star Trek* story. I confess that the most fun for me was planning the space battles. Imagine yourself in my position: you get to sit in Captain Picard's chair and make the *Enterprise* do anything you have ever wanted it to do! I always wanted to see the *Enterprise* flip upside down and fire her lateral phasers. I always wanted to see the *Enterprise* roll completely over and go to emergency warp. In *Nemesis*, she does.

Shinzon, the Romulans, and the Remans

Without a doubt, the single most important part of developing the story was creating our villain. We knew from *Khan* and *First Contact* that *Trek* works best when the hero has a *personal* relationship with the villain. Because of their history, Kirk has a strong, emotional connection to Khan. Because of his history Picard has a strong, emotional connection to the Borg. We knew Picard must have a deep and personal response to whomever our antagonist was going to be. From the beginning we wanted a young, sexy male enemy because we haven't seen that before in one of the movies.

And we wanted the Romulans.

My theory is that there are two kinds of *Star Trek* fans: Romulan people and Klingon people. I am very much a

Romulan person. All that wild, unrestrained machismo of our friends from Qo'noS isn't as interesting to me as the lethal machinations of the Romulans. For a writer, the malicious subtlety of the Romulans offers great opportunities; the cleverness and formality of their language must suggest that they are simultaneously a deadly political foe and a noble, ancient race. Besides, I had just finished working on *Gladiator* and was in a classical frame of mind. The serpentine rhythms of the language we created for the Roman Empire in that movie were good practice for writing the august and treacherous Romulans.

And haven't you always wondered about Remus? Two planets make up the homeworlds of the Empire—we see them both in the familiar Romulan bird-of-prey symbol—but Remus has been almost unmentioned. Here is where being a fan paid off.

Another typical exchange:

JOHN

Now, we want a new race. Something really scary. Okay, get this . . . how about we use . . . (terribly excited) . . . *the Remans!*

RICK

What's a Reman?

BRENT

Are those the blue guys with the antennae?

JOHN

No, no, no, those are the *Andorians!* Do you guys ever actually *watch* the show?!

Introduction

RICK

Okay, so tell us about the Remans...

Brent and Rick agreed it would be fun to explore the Remans and their relation to the Romulans. The idea of the Remans being vampirelike slaves, laboring away in the dilithium mines, never seeing the sun, grew out of our desire to create a truly monstrous race. It seemed obvious to me that the Romulans would subjugate some other race to dig dilithium for them. Much too messy for our pristine and elegant Romulans.

Our villain, Shinzon, actually began the long road to his final incarnation in *Nemesis* as Picard's long-lost *son*. We explored this avenue for a while but kept crashing into brick walls. Where has this son been? How did he end up with the Romulans? Why hasn't Picard ever mentioned him? Can we do something that runs so contrary to Picard's established history? For session after session we tried to figure out clever ways to get around all this. No use. Here's a piece of advice for all you writers out there: When you keep running into a brick wall, don't just try to paint the wall different colors, demolish it.

It was Rick who finally demolished the wall. He came to the rescue with the single idea that galvanized the whole story: have the villain be Picard's *clone*. Rick argued persuasively that it would be more compelling to have Picard versus Picard. What better adversary than yourself? What better foe than a man who thinks just like you do, with the same strengths and weaknesses? What could be more poignant for Captain Picard than facing a dark mirror of himself?

To a writer, this was irresistible. I could explore a character with as much depth as Picard himself. I could write him with the same sort of dynamic language that Picard employs. I knew Shinzon, like Picard, would have to be eloquent and smart. And he would have to be *complex*. We wanted a multidimensional antagonist who truly believes he is doing the right thing for his people. When we were creating Shinzon, we talked a lot about John Brown, the nineteenth century abolitionist. John Brown was not a slave, but he went to war, and eventually died, fighting to free the slaves. He was a violently passionate zealot. So too is Shinzon. He truly believes he is fighting to free his Reman "brothers."

(By the way, "Shinzon" and all the Reman and Romulan names in the story are based on ancient Chinese names. This was our way of paying homage to Gene Roddenberry's original idea that the Romulans represented the 1960's Chinese Communists.)

Writing the Script

After about a year of meeting with Rick and Brent and hammering out the story, I went away and wrote the first draft of the actual script. The Okudas' *Star Trek Encyclopedia* and Larry Nemecek's *Star Trek: The Next Generation Companion* were always at my side. Don't even think about seriously diving into *Trek* without them.

But before I put finger to keyboard, I watched the entire *Next Generation* series over again. (And they pay me for this!) I wanted to get the character's voices firmly in my head. Exploring these unique voices, and trying to get them right, was one of the most rewarding challenges of the whole *Nemesis* experience. Since I have spent so much time with our crew over the years, I had a feel for how they might express themselves in dialogue: Data has his slightly odd, formal language with unexpected flourishes; Riker is more fun and breezy, always ready with a wry observation; Deanna's language ebbs and flows in gentle rhythms; Geordi is the most casual and accessible; etc.

The biggest challenge was Picard. Because I have so much respect for the character, it was a little intimidating trying to find his voice. I had to try to capture his intelligence, his innate morality and his hopeful spirit.

Here I give all credit to the splendid Patrick Stewart for helping me along. Rick and I met with Patrick a number of times while I was working on various drafts, and he was always patient and encouraging. He pushed me to go deeper and make Picard's language rise to the occasion. When in doubt, Rick and I would ask him to extemporize, to play around with the wording of a particular scene as Picard might. Patrick happily obliged as I scribbled down his words. Some of Picard's best dialogue in the movie comes directly from those impromptu sessions. Patrick was also invaluable in helping me examine the depth of Picard's emotional response to Shinzon. After spending all those years with the good captain, Patrick brought shrewd and provocative insights into how Picard might respond in a given circumstance. To use an unforgivable cliché, Patrick was, and is, a joy to work with.

Once Picard's language began to fall into place, Shinzon's language followed. I wanted Shinzon to echo Picard in his rhythms of speech. I tried throughout the script to have Shinzon mirror the cadences of Picard's dialogue, actually counting syllables to try to make an almost subconscious lingual connection between the two characters.

I wrote the first draft in about five weeks, working nonstop in a sort of frenzied rush to get it all down on the page. It was like an exorcism: over thirty years of dreaming about *Trek* cascading out of me in a furious spasm of writing. I sent the first draft to Rick and then escaped to Death Valley for a week to walk around the desert and recover.

About sixteen drafts followed in happy succession over the next year. With each draft, Rick would patiently roll up his sleeves and dive in with me to help make it better. We debated and discussed and tweaked and shaped. We acted out the scenes and used whatever was handy in his office to choreograph the ship battles. We worked through each and every draft page by page, often line by line.

It was heaven.

Trust me, a screenwriter doesn't usually get that kind of detailed attention. Rick is as much of a compulsive workaholic as I am and he made himself available to me twenty-four hours a day, seven days a week. We talked constantly and his family was extraordinarily patient when I would bug him at all hours to discuss some tiny detail of Shinzon's background or the geography of Remus of the photon torpedo complement of the *Enterprise*-E.

When the final draft of *Nemesis* was done, the budgeting process began. Inevitably, the movie was going to be expensive, the elaborate Third Act battle sequence assured it. Working closely with our director, Stuart Baird, we began making cuts. Some of the cuts were just trims to bring the movie down to a manageable length and others were made so we wouldn't break the bank. Remember, every time you see stars outside a window it is an expensive optical effect. Every time you see a phaser or disruptor beam it is a visual effect. Every time you see a Reman it is elaborate and costly makeup.

During all this, Rick was courageous in protecting the integrity of the script. We discussed every single cut and considered every possible option. In the end, I think the only element we both regret having to lose was a subplot involving Worf. In the earlier drafts we spent more time exploring his complex relationship with the Romulans; how they butchered his parents at Khitomer, etc. Worf's Third Act battle with the Reman invaders on the *Enterprise* was originally longer and he concluded the story being saved by a *Romulan* doctor. Sadly, we had to lose much of this.

The final movie very much reflects what I wrote. I certainly worked diligently to try to write an exciting *Trek* movie, a movie for the fans, but I must finally give the credit to my wonderful collaborators. Brent was simply invaluable during the development of the script. Patrick was a prince in helping me to understand Picard. Stuart Baird, the whole production team, and all the actors labored incredibly hard to bring the story to you with passion and honesty. And Rick Berman tenderly nurtured every single aspect of the movie for two years running.

Rick may not know what a Reman is, but he is this *Trek*'s fan hero.

A Final Thought

One of my fondest memories of the whole *Nemesis* experience was when I met Jonathan Frakes for the first time. He came up to me and shook my hand with that big, warm smile of his and said, "Welcome to the family."

Introduction

It was an extremely moving moment for me.

But then I have been a member of this family for over thirty years, from the first time I met Captain Kirk when I was a kid. Anyone who has found pleasure and solace and inspiration from the *Trek* saga is a member of the family.

You are too.

STAR TREK®
nemesis

Prologue

In the vast Senate chamber, Hiren, praetor and ultimate ruler of the entire Romulan Star Empire, sat in his great chair, which some derisively called a throne. The society in which he lived had for millennia been militarized, urban; even so, the tides of nature were tied strongly to the Romulan being. Beyond these vast, ancient walls, Hiren knew, the red Romulan sun was slipping below the horizon, infusing the sky, buildings, and glittering skimmers with an ethereal crimson glow.

A sudden urge overtook him—to desert the chamber, to leave the pontificating senators agape, to board his own sleek skimmer and flee the city that was the crowning glory of the Empire. To return to the comfort of home: and then he remembered that there was no comfort there, only silence and solitude. His wife T'Shara, one of the highest-ranking commanders in the military, was to have returned home from the Celesian campaign this day, and been waiting for him this night. T'Shara, the only one from whom he feared no treachery, the only one against whom he

1

need not scheme. She had been killed two days before by one of her own centurions, who had mistaken her for the enemy.

The centurion, of course, had been quickly executed; but in this case revenge brought Hiren no relief. He was not a young man—his hair had silvered many seasons ago—but neither was he old. Yet today he had complained to his physician of aches and pains befitting one twice his age. T'Shara had taken with her into the afterworld his life, his heart, his will. His passion for power and scheming had deserted him: all that was left now was a hollow sense of duty.

His personal guards and those loyal to him in the Senate and military pled desperately with him to shake off his listlessness, to remain alert: He would need every ounce of his shrewdness, his cunning, to save the Empire from being torn apart by the creature known as Shinzon. The praetor's life was endangered now more than at any other time during his rule: Did he not care? Grieve for T'Shara later, at a safer time. For now, there was duty.

Duty . . . A dry, empty word that to Hiren's tongue tasted of dust. Yet, for the sake of the Empire—and because T'Shara would have wanted him to—he gathered what was left of his concentration and resolve and applied his attention to the task at hand.

The Senate chamber was filled to capacity: The very air seemed to vibrate, electric with the curiosity of a hundred senators eager—even desperate—to hear the arguments for and against the Reman leader, Shinzon, who had suggested an extremely radical approach to dealing with the Federation. But it would require the Empire to provide military support to the Remans and treat them as equals, which they were not.

A vote had already been taken: By a narrow margin—too narrow for Hiren's comfort—the Senate had voted against

Shinzon. But the praetor alone had the final say, and he had let no one know of his decision.

The military, of course, was divided, which meant the resolution of the situation was critical to Hiren's survival, both as praetor and a living being. Hiren had not attained the highest political position in the Empire by being innocent or trusting. Before news of T'Shara's death arrived, he had already determined which among the Senate and military supported him, and threatened or bribed those who did not. He feared neither the Reman leader, nor the commanders who came to the podium and began their arguments on Shinzon's behalf.

The younger commander—Talik, was it?—was filled with typical youthful impatience; there was anger in his tone, which provoked Hiren to glare threateningly at him.

Talik gesticulated with his arms, muscles rippling beneath the sleeves of his uniform. "What you don't seem to understand is that this is a chance to make ourselves stronger than ever before! I beg you not to let prejudice or politics interfere with this alliance!"

Prejudice, Hiren thought bitterly, and for an instant, directed his gaze at the facing wall. Above the seated senator, the great crest of the Empire hung, a stylized image of Romulus's most famous bird of prey, grasping in each talon a planet—one light, one dark. Romulus and Remus—twins, but not equals, for while Romulus enjoyed a regular night and day, Remus was placed too close to the sun. Half of the planet baked constantly, a sere, unlivable desert; half remained in constant night, and on that half, the population dwelled, and over time had evolved into hideous, light-blinded creatures. The Remans had already proven themselves inferior by living for centuries as slaves

3

under Romulan rule. Had they been worthy of the rights and status accorded Romulans, they would have fought for them. Such was the Romulan way: The strong conquered, and the weak were enslaved. Hiren would not see the great Empire plunged into night.

Commander Bezor, an older and wiser Romulan whom Hiren had known—and up to this moment, respected—for many years, made a gesture of supplication toward the praetor's throne, which also served to silence the young Talik.

"Praetor," he said, his tone placating. "Senators . . . What my colleague is saying is that Shinzon represents an *opportunity* for the Empire. If handled properly, he and his people can heighten our own glory."

Talik failed to restrain himself. "It's already too late to go back. We must move forward *together*! And when his forces join ours, not even the Federation will be able to stand in our way—!"

Hiren gripped the armrests of his chair, feigning indignation at Talik's impudence and Bezor's betrayal. *"Enough!"* he snapped. *"The decision has been made!"* He paused, gathered himself, and in a cooler voice said, "The military does not dictate policy on Romulus. The Senate has considered Shinzon's proposal and rejected it. He and his followers will be met with all deliberate force and sent back to that black rock they came from. Do I make myself clear?"

The young Commander Talik stood, silently defiant; Bezor was wise enough to bow his head and say graciously, "Praetor."

"The subcommittee on military affairs will be meeting tomorrow to prepare our tactical response," Hiren told him. "You will attend." For the praetor would be sure to give Bezor an assignment that would test his loyalty; if he failed, Bezor would be swiftly executed. If he proved loyal, then he would be required to surrender all knowledge of the foe. The young Talik's fate was already decided.

Bezor seemed sincerely grateful for the opportunity to redeem himself—but Hiren had met too many excellent liars in his day to be overwhelmed with trust. "Yes, sir," the older commander said, with another slight bow, then turned and left the chamber. Commander Talik followed, fuming.

With the departure of the two men, it was as though gravity itself eased slightly; Hiren waited for the subtle whispering of bodies turning in their chairs and the murmurs of senators commenting to their fellows to die down before he spoke again.

This time he addressed Trann, a Romulan male who had been in the Senate long before Hiren danced in his mother's womb. "Now, Senator," Hiren said with near-courtesy, "you were speaking of a trade affiliation with Celes Two?"

Old Trann rose and nodded, his dark eyes veiled by heavy white eyebrows. "Yes, Praetor. The trade committee has concluded that an agreement is in the best interests of the Empire. We recommend dispatching a diplomatic mission to open negotiations."

At the word *negotiations*, the senator beside Trann grunted. Hiren heard the skepticism that laced the small sound, and turned his full attention to her: Senator Tal'Aura, quite young and handsome, in the most classic Romulan way. Black hair with glints of blue, fierce, upward-arching brows above black eyes, and an intangible aura of coiled passion. She had risen to the position of senator at an extraordinarily early age out of determination and intelligence: someday she would no doubt be praetor. Before his heart died two days before, Hiren had suggested a political and romantic alliance—but Tal'Aura had found a way to refuse him without sparking his ire. Her politics, it seemed, were marked by the skepticism of youth. The Celesian system was currently at the Empire's mercy, and was hardly in a position to truly bargain. She was simply expressing the truth in a sigh, yet he could not let a discourtesy to Senator Trann pass so easily.

"Senator Tal'Aura," Hiren said sternly. "You disagree with the motion?"

She faced him boldly. "No, sir. I would say 'negotiation' is to be advised. I support all 'diplomatic' overtures. But if you will excuse me, Praetor, I have an appointment with the Tholian ambassador."

Hiren knew her latter statement to be true, so he nodded, dismissing her; she rose and quickly exited the chamber. Before he glanced away, Hiren noted that she left behind a small silver box, intricately engraved—a gift, no doubt, from another political admirer hoping for a liaison. He would have one of his own guards retrieve it after the session, in order to learn with whom she might be allying herself these days.

Then, for duty's sake, he forced himself to continue the session. "Then I will call for a vote," Praetor Hiren said, "on the motion to open trade negotiations with Celes Two."

As he spoke, he became aware that the silver box was *moving*, its top panels folding out, opening like a flower to the sun. From its center, a double-helix of pure, swirling energy grew slowly; and when it had reached full height, a pulse of bright green light began to climb up the helix.

In the first instant, its beauty convinced Hiren that it was piece of artwork, inadvertently activated; in the next, his politican's brain convinced him that Tal'Aura's loyalty to the Empire was shakier and her thirst for power greater than he had allowed himself to imagine. She had not left this "gift" behind unintentionally—it had been meant specifically for him, and it had come from Shinzon.

When the pulse of energy reached the top of the helix, a beam of green light shot straight up to the high-domed ceiling, then cascaded down like a waterfall, like a glowing emerald mist, enshrouding the entire chamber and its inhabitants. A few of the senators gasped in surprise, but all soon fell into an awed silence.

It was really quite beautiful, Hiren decided; had death been this beautiful for his wife, T'Shara? Death by disruptor was supposedly quite painful—but had there been an instant for her like this one, when her entire being was absorbed by radiance, as each cell was lit up from within?

The glow evaporated suddenly. Just as suddenly, Hiren contemplated the great bird of prey on the wall, and the dark planet, Remus, in its grip. Outside, sunset had just given way to night, and he realized the irony Shinzon intended: The Empire, indeed, was being plunged into Reman darkness.

Yet even as Hiren's mind watched with an observer's detachment in his final moments, his body and brain continued to react with the habit of duty. T'Shara would have done the same. "Would someone please tell me what that was?" he asked, then turned to a guard. "Alert security . . ."

But he knew it was already too late, for a glance behind him showed that the flowering plant behind him was drooping, shriveling. Dying. Still, he continued giving orders: duty before death.

". . . and have them run a . . ."

Hiren could say no more, for the flesh of his tongue began to melt away; and as he watched the yellow-green flesh dissolve from the guard's face, giving way to muscle and blood beneath, he saw his own countenance mirrored. The dissolution of cells was excruciating, beyond bearing, and he could not have said whether the short-lived screams that sounded in his ears were his own or those of others around him.

He only knew this: that T'Shara had experienced both, the beauty and the agony of dying; and the last bit of light Hiren saw with his liquefying eyes was the shimmer of a transporter beam as the silver box, the weapon, was removed from the chamber.

And then there was nothing but darkness. Darkness, and stillness, and the silence of eternal Reman night.

Chapter 1

Worlds away, on the planet Earth in the area known as Alaska, Captain Jean-Luc Picard rose from the table at which he sat, and for a moment, gazed beyond the people gathered before him at his magnificent surroundings: the Denali mountain range, snow-capped against a blue sky. The open-air pavilion was heated to a comfortable temperature, but on occasion, Picard drew in a breath of cold, pristine oxygen tinged with evergreen.

The natural beauty only added to the poignancy of the moment: to gather himself, Picard concentrated on the discomfort generated by his white-dress jacket, the white tunic beneath fitted tightly at the neck, and kept his expression resolute, even stern.

"Duty," he intoned, to the officers at the bride and groom's table with him. To his right sat Beverly; to his left, Will Riker and Deanna Troi, flanked by Geordi, Data, and Worf. In front of the large, central table were dozens of smaller ones, occupied by other crewmates and friends. "A starship captain's life is filled with solemn duty. I have commanded men in battle. I have negotiated peace treaties between implacable enemies. I have represented the Federation in first contact with twenty-

9

seven alien species. But none of this compares to my solemn duty as . . ." He paused for effect. "Best man."

From their center seats at the table, Will and Deanna laughed along with the rest of the guests—all except Data, who watched the ritual with avid curiosity. Deanna's skin seemed to radiate the precise color of her gown—iridescent pale rose, gleaming like a newfound pearl. Quite a bit of skin there was, too, with the low-cut, sleeveless bodice, but her legs were covered by the sweeping skirt. One shoulder bore a corsage of cabbage roses; a cascade of roses swirled about the skirt from waist to hem.

A pink pearl, Picard thought, amidst a sea of white and gray uniforms; all officers other than the captain wore gray tunics beneath their white dress jackets.

He continued to feign sternness, though his mood was a mixture of joy and melancholy. "Now, I know that on an occasion such as this it is expected that I be gracious and fulsome with praise on the wonders of this blessed union . . . But have you two considered what you're doing to *me?* Of course *you're* happy! But what about *my* needs?! This is all a damned inconven-ience . . ." He continued despite the crowd's laughter. "While you're happily settling in on the *Titan*, I'll have to train my new first officer. You all know him. He's a steely sort of fellow who knows every word of every paragraph of every regulation by heart; a stern martinet who will never, ever, allow me to go on away missions."

He glanced at the golden-faced android, Data, who looked up at him with those peculiarly guileless eyes. "That is the regulation, sir," Data said earnestly. "Starfleet Code section twelve, paragraph four—"

"Data," Picard countered, in a more casual tone.

"Sir?"

"Shut up."

More laughter came from the crowd, especially Deanna, whose dark hair was swept up into a graceful chignon. Picard turned his sights on her and affected his best curmudgeonly tone.

"Then there's the matter of my new counselor," he said. "No doubt they'll assign me some soft-spoken, willowy thing who'll probe into my darkest psyche as she nods her head and coos sympathetically. Isn't that right, Deanna?"

The broad grin disappeared from Deanna's face; instead, she conjured a wide-eyed, strikingly concerned expression and cooed—sympathetically, of course. Beverly, who had served as matron of honor, leaned toward her laughingly and clapped.

"I notice Doctor Crusher laughing along with the rest of you," Picard continued. "As most of you know, the doctor will also soon be leaving the *Enterprise,* to assume command of Starfleet Medical." He spread his hands in mock supplication. "Again, I'm forced to ask, Beverly, have you considered what you're doing to *me?* I'll probably get some old battle-axe of a doctor who'll tell me to eat my vegetables and put me on report if I don't show up for my physical on time."

"It'll serve you right," Beverly called back spiritedly.

Picard sighed and regarded Will and Deanna again. "Really, it's not too late to reconsider . . ." And when they both, grinning, shook their heads, he added, "No? Very well then." At last, he surrendered his sarcastic tone, raised his glass, and smiled affectionately at the two.

"Will Riker," he said. "You have been my trusted right arm for fifteen years, you have helped keep my course true and steady." He paused to gaze at the bride. "Deanna Troi, you have been my conscience and guide, you have helped me to recognize the best parts of myself." To both he said, "You are my family. And in proper maritime tradition, I wish you clear horizons . . . My friends, make it so."

Picard and the rest of those gathered upended their glasses.

A band had begun to play, and the guests to mingle; Picard began to make his way toward Riker and Crusher, but in midstride he paused once again to take in the three-hundred-and-sixty-degree sight of the Denali range, framed at its base by stands of tall evergreens. The mountains, white set against glistening white, formed a jagged horizon against the clear Earth-blue sky. They appeared permanent, eternal: but in spring, Picard knew, their collective face would change; great patches of white would give way to dark earth and dark greenery, giving a dappled light-and-shadow effect.

The more things change, the more they stay the same, his brother Robert had always said, but Picard saw no validity in the statement—especially not on this day. Things were changing, quite radically in fact, and he failed to see how his life would ever be the same.

Beverly Crusher appeared before him—much older than on the day they first met, something less of a mystery, but certainly no less beautiful, with her red-gold hair that seemed a reflection of her warm personality. His maudlin thought must have affected his expression, for she picked up on his feelings at once and teased, "Sort of like losing a son and gaining an empath, isn't it?"

Picard grimaced sourly at her. "You're being a big help."

She put a hand lightly on the crook of his elbow and said

playfully into his ear, "If you start tearing up I promise to beam you out. Level one medical emergency."

He had to smile at that. As the two of them made their way through the crowd toward Will and Deanna, young Wesley Crusher—surprisingly mature-looking in a Starfleet lieutenant's uniform—crossed their path.

Wesley grinned broadly. "Mom!" Then, with a more formal air as he straightened his shoulders, added: "Captain."

"Hello, Wesley," Picard said easily. "It's good to see you back in uniform."

"Suits him, doesn't it?" Beverly said. She was suddenly incandescent with pride; Picard tried to imagine what it would have been like to raise a child, then finally see him one day grown and in uniform, and felt the stirrings of wistful jealousy. There were many paths he had chosen not to take in his life—children included—and Beverly's proximity served to remind him of other lost opportunities.

Nevertheless, he returned Wesley's grin. "Are you looking forward to serving on the *Titan?*"

Lieutenant Crusher's words tumbled out with the enthusiasm of youth. "Very much. I have the night duty shift in engineering, we have a double-refracting warp core matrix with twin inter-mix chambers that . . ." He stopped abruptly, his attention seized by the appearance of a young woman who waved in his direction. "Oh, excuse me. See you later, Mom."

At once he was off, in pursuit of the girl. Picard could only smile and gently shake his head at the fleeting attention span of youth; had he ever really been that young? Beverly's smile was a bit more rueful.

Once again, they headed for Troi and Riker.

• • •

Nearby, Engineer Geordi La Forge sat at the bar nursing a glass of synthehol while talking with Guinan. Like most of his crewmates, he was in a state of near-shock: Troi and Riker had been an item years before they worked together on the *Enterprise,* and for their several years as crewmates, they had remained good friends, nothing more. (Although, of course, LaForge had always known Will Riker was still carrying feelings for Deanna.) Then the courtship began anew—but the notion that the couple might actually make their relationship more permanent—well, it just seemed like one of those things crew members liked to speculate about, but which would never happen, rather like Captain Picard suddenly professing love for Dr. Crusher.

La Forge shook his head, laughing. "I still can't believe he finally popped the question!"

Ever-serene and self-confident, Guinan leaned forward to prop her elbows against the bar. "What makes you so sure *he* popped the question?"

"Counselor Troi?" Geordi set down his flute and raised his eyebrows. "You gotta be kidding." He had always thought of Commander Riker being the one to pursue Troi, of Riker having to convince Troi to love him—but perhaps he, Geordi, had always thought of things that way because he was male, and it always seemed to him that he had to work to earn a female's affection. Or did the insecurity work both ways?

"You have to keep an eye on us quiet, soulful types," Guinan said mysteriously, her lips curving upward in the small smile-that-was-not-quite-a-smile.

Her answer gave Geordi a thought, and that thought made him grin. "You ever think about getting married again?"

Guinan looked past him, at the Alaskan skyline, her voice trailing. "Maybe . . ." And then her gaze and voice promptly returned. "But like I always say, why buy the Denubian sea-cow when you can get the milk for free?"

Geordi barely snickered, then picked up his glass; as he did, the Klingon Worf sat heavily, with a slight groan, on the stool beside him. The normally bronze skin beneath Worf's eyes was ashen, his thick eyebrows knit together beneath his bony forehead, which was furrowed even more deeply than usual. The Klingon had continued to let his hair grow, and now wore it in a simple braid down his back.

"Romulan ale should be illegal," Worf rasped. He referred, of course, to Riker's bachelor party, held the night before: the Klingon had been less than circumspect in his imbibing.

Geordi dared not smile, but he did allow himself the comment, "It is."

"Then it should be more illegal," Worf said with conviction. He groaned—loudly this time—and set his head down on the table while Geordi and Guinan shared a knowing glance.

Meanwhile, Picard and Crusher had at last made their way to Will Riker and Deanna Troi.

Troi smiled warmly at Picard with her ebony eyes, and touched his forearm with her hand. "It was a lovely toast."

"It was from the heart," Picard said honestly.

"And you needn't worry," Deanna added. "I'll brief your new counselor on everything she needs to know."

"The hell you will," the captain replied with gruff humor. "You already know too much about me. Now you promised there are no speeches during the ceremony on Betazed."

Will and Deanna shared a bemused look. *Should I remind him?* Will's expression asked, and Deanna's said, *Go ahead.*

"No, no speeches," Riker said, failing entirely to hide the impishness in his eyes. "No clothes, either."

Picard gave him a sharp look—apparently he'd assumed that non-Betazoid guests were exempt from this traditional marital ritual—but his former second-in-command wasn't joking, even though his new wife laughed at Picard's reaction.

Before Picard could come up with a witty reply, the band stopped playing; at the sound of Data's voice, all turned to face the bandstand.

"Ladies and gentlemen and invited transgendered species . . . In my study of Terran and Betazoid conjugal rites I have discovered it is traditional to present the 'happy couple' with a gift. Given Commander Riker's affection for archaic musical forms I have elected to present the following as my gift in honor of their conjugation."

Will shot Deanna an amused glance. *Conjugation?*

Data began to recite a verse; gradually, the band joined in.

> "Never saw the sun
> Shining so bright,
> Never saw things
> Going so right,
> Noticing the days
> Hurrying by-
> When you're in love,
> My how they fly!"

The band launched full voice into a style that Picard recognized as twentieth-century Earth swing. Data began to sing:

"Blue skies
  Smiling at me,
  Nothing but blue skies
  Do I see.
  Bluebirds
  Singing a song,
  Nothing but bluebirds
  All day long."

The rhythm was irresistible—to all except Worf, who raised his head from the table and groaned loudly over the music, "Ugghhh . . . Irving Berlin." And with a great thump, his head struck the table again. Picard turned away to hide his smile; he had left Will's bachelor party early, lest his presence inhibit any of the celebrating, but by that time, Mr. Worf had already imbibed enough Romulan ale to account for his current condition.

Beside the captain, Will was tapping his foot to the beat; the groom gave his bride an anxious little glance, like a child asking permission to go join the fun.

Deanna smiled at him indulgently. "All right, go ahead."

Riker ran up onto the bandstand, where his trombone rested off to the side; he grabbed it and began playing.

Picard turned to Deanna and proffered a white-sleeved arm. "May I have this dance?"

She grinned. "With pleasure, Captain."

They swirled out onto the dance floor.

Meantime, Beverly Crusher took pity on Worf's misery and decided to distract him from it. The Klingon could very well have come to sickbay and asked for treatment which would have gotten rid of his apparent hangover—but perhaps Worf would have considered such help a sign of weakness.

Besides, Crusher hadn't seen him in some time and would not see him again for—well, at the very least, years, and quite possibly forever. She had teased Jean-Luc Picard about becoming emotional at this wedding reception—but she may as well have been talking to herself. It had been hard enough when Wesley left the *Enterprise* years ago, but now she was leaving; leaving Jean-Luc and Will and Deanna all at once, and the sense of loss was staggering. There had been a time, when she had first been offered the position of head of Starfleet Medical, that she had actually considered turning it down. Her life was on the *Enterprise,* she had told herself; she had made deep ties with many people here—so deep that she considered them as much her family as her own son.

But the more she considered the offer from Starfleet, the more she realized she could not turn it down. She was a seasoned space traveler, but there had been times, especially in the past few years, when her longing for home—for Earth—became overwhelming. Soon it became persistent—and then the current head of Medical announced his retirement.

Beverly applied for the position, with Picard's recommendation to back her. The process of applying, of the interviews, sparked a deep determination within her. She had spent the past fifteen years as a doctor aboard a starship—indeed, as the chief medical officer of the Fleet's most prominent, prestigious starship. But the good that she could do aboard the *Enterprise* was far different from the far-reaching type of good she could do at Starfleet Medical . . . and she was ready for a difference, for a new challenge.

Yet now, walking across the dance floor toward Worf, Crusher suddenly asked herself, *Can I really leave these people?*

She chided herself for being overly sentimental. She had a promotion, a new job and new friends to make. Now was the time for celebrating, not grieving. It was beautiful here, with the glittery snowy mountains and the deep blue sky, the good friends, and the music . . .

As Beverly walked toward Worf, she passed a smiling Geordi La Forge, who was leading a beautiful African woman in a brilliant red dress to the dance floor. Apparently they knew each other more than well—*that* was something she was going to have to Deanna about, to get the ship's latest buzz.

Beverly walked up behind the stool where the Klingon sat, slumped facedown on the table, and said in the loudest, most determinedly cheerful voice she could muster, "Commander Worf. Do Klingons swing?"

"I am unwell," he muttered into the table.

"Don't worry, I'm a doctor." With all her strength, she took hold of one of his massive arms and pulled him off the table and onto his feet. He staggered slightly as she drew him onto the floor, among the gliding bodies, and as he attempted to mimic her movements, it was clear he had little familiarity with the style of dance known as swing. Even so, he managed admirably, taking her fine-boned pale hand in his great dark one with a light touch.

"I'm so glad you made it back to the *Enterprise* before I left," she called over the din of the music. To her, dance came naturally; her bones were long and fine, her muscles limber and blessed with that mystery known as a sense of rhythm. She could scarcely have resisted dragging the Klingon onto the floor even if he'd been unconscious.

Worf's pained expression eased slightly; it was the closest he would come to acknowledging mutual affection. To those unfamiliar with Klingons, he would have seemed ferocious, with the great jutting browbone above narrowed eyes and jagged teeth; to Beverly he looked precious. "I was not suited for the life of a . . . diplomat."

An understatement if ever there was one. She managed not to laugh aloud at the thought, but instead twisted her lips wryly and shrugged. "Who'd have guessed?"

At that instant, Picard and Deanna, talking and grinning, went dancing past them; Beverly looked at them both, and at Worf, and thought: *I must remember every little detail of this moment, of this time. I must remember . . .*

As she moved amidst the swirling bodies, with the backdrop of the Alaskan skyline, the moment seemed to her at once timeless and fleeting, a celebration of the brevity of life against the eternal snow-clad mountains. It seemed to her that she had been on the *Enterprise,* friend and fellow crew member to these people, for all of her life—yet now that she was leaving them, it seemed the experience had been all too short, that her moments with them had been too few.

Beverly let her gaze focus on those she loved around her: on Worf, on Data singing on the stage, at the trombone-wielding Will Riker, like Deanna radiant with joy. *If only this moment could last forever . . .*

Yet in the midst of a longing that verged on grief, Beverly could not hold back a smile.

Later that night, in his quarters aboard the *Enterprise,* Picard gingerly withdrew a bottle from his temperature- and humidity-controlled wine storage unit. He had to half-kneel to do so, and the gesture seemed appropriate, in light of the value—not just monetarily, but historically and emotionally—of the liquid inside. He held the bottle up to the light: its contents were the deep color of garnet, and the glass, plain breakable glass which was no longer used to house such fine wine, glinted jewel-like.

He rose, the glass cool in his hands, and stepped forward into the outer area, where Data sat at the table, gently turning the captain's Ressikan flute in his hands—studying it, digesting it, head slightly cocked. The android's expression seemed entirely neutral . . . and yet, Picard thought, Data's amber eyes somehow managed to convey a sense of wonder, of curiosity that was entirely human.

Picard gestured slightly, carefully, with the wine, cheered to have someone to share it with who would truly appreciate the experience. "I've been saving this," he said heartily. "Chateau Picard 2267 . . . Batten down the hatches." Deliberately, he began to uncork the bottle; Data looked up with the same expression of placid yet somehow voracious curiosity and listened intently as Picard continued, "They say a vintner's history is in every glass. The soil he came from. His past as well as his hopes for the future . . ."

As the cork slipped past the lip of the bottle, a heavenly aroma followed: cassis, cherry, grape, and herb and rich earth. Picard's vintner's nose knew at once the ratio of sugar to acid was perfect, the wine neither too young nor too old, but exactly in its prime. Set on the table were two wine glasses; Picard filled each one-quarter full, then slipped his fingers beneath the bowl of one, supporting the stem with his middle and ring finger, and handed it to Data.

Data held it awkwardly by the stem, but corrected himself at once when he saw that Picard held his own glass with all of his fingers supporting the bowl. Red wine should be gently warmed by the heat of the body.

Picard smiled affectionately as he lifted his glass. "So . . . To the future."

"To the future," Data echoed.

Through the wine and the crystal, Picard watched his soon-to-be first officer imitate his every move: Take a small sip. Let the liquid rest a moment on the tongue, enjoy the burst of different flavors there, savor the ever-changing aftertaste. At last release the breath, in a satisfied, delighted, "Ah . . ."

Picard regarded the android with amused affection.

"Sir," Data said solemnly as he lowered his glass, "I noticed an interesting confluence of emotion at the wedding. I am familiar with the human concept of tears through laughter and its inverse, laughter through tears, but I could not help wondering about the human capacity for expressing both pleasure and sadness simultaneously."

"I understand why it would seem confusing," Picard replied. To some, perhaps, Data's ingenuous yet perplexing questions might be cause for irritation, yet the captain had always been grateful for them; they served to help him crystallize his own feelings, to make what was often unconscious conscious. "Certain human rituals—like weddings, birthdays, or funerals—evoke strong and very complex emotions because they mark important transitions in our lives."

Data tilted his head every so slightly, a gesture that always accompanied his attempt to fathom humankind. "They denote the passage of time."

"More than that," Picard elaborated. "In a way, they make us aware of our mortality. These occasions give us an opportunity to think about where we've been and where we're going." The sense of melancholy he'd felt during the wedding reception threatened to settle upon him again.

"And you were particularly aware of this feeling of 'transition' because Commander Riker will be leaving to assume command of the *Titan?*"

Picard nodded, his focus shifting to a point beyond Data, beyond the physical limits of his quarters, to a place in the future. "Will and Deanna joining the *Titan* . . . Dr. Crusher going to Starfleet Medical . . ."

"And this makes you 'sad'?" Data emphasized the word in his effort to define it.

Picard drew in a breath and with it, shifted his attention from what would be to what was. He smiled wistfully at the android. "Well . . . I suppose it does a bit. I'm very happy for them, of course, but I'm going to miss them. The ship will seem . . . incomplete without them."

Data gave a short nod, as if satisfied that he was finally able to understand this complex mix of emotion. "That is because you have a familiarity with them. You can predict specific reactions and behavior and are comfortable in that knowledge."

"Yes," Picard admitted. "And, frankly, I envy them as well. They've made important choices; choices that mean life will be different from now on. They're going to have great challenges ahead of them. New worlds to conquer . . ." He paused to take another sip of wine, to relish the product of his past, and that of his forebears, before glancing at the Ressikan flute resting near Data.

"Seeing Will and Deanna today made me think about some of the choices I've made in my own life," he said, and thought of the moment he'd stood beside Beverly at the reception and watched the light that had entered her eyes when she'd looked at her son. "Devoting myself to Starfleet . . . Not marrying or having children . . . All the choices that led me here."

Data remained silent a moment before at last saying slowly: "The choices I made have led me here as well. This is the only home I have ever known. I cannot foresee a reason for leaving."

"You never know what's over the horizon, Data," the captain warned lightly. "Before too long you'll be offered a command of your own."

Data glanced at him sharply; Picard marveled at the realization that such a notion had never occurred to the android. "If I were," Data countered, "I believe my memory engrams would sense the absence of your specific reactions and behavior. I would 'miss you.' "

Touched, Picard smiled and lifted his own glass. "Now, you make a toast."

Data raised his glass. "To . . ." He hesitated, for a moment at a loss—then added confidently, ". . . new worlds."

"New worlds," Picard echoed.

They both put the glasses to their lips and drank.

Chapter 2

The high ceilings and ancient walls of Senate corridors were still draped in Reman night, eased only by the flickering red glow of braziers that had, until now, remained unlit for millennia, a reminder of Romulus's deep past.

It was as though, Commander Donatra thought, she were walking back through history, into a dark time when the Senate had not been a political forum where disputes were aired, but an arena where they were settled publicly, with blades and bloodstains long faded now from the Chamber floor. True, the machinations of Romulan politics were still vicious enough, with those choosing the wrong alliance sometimes disappearing more cleanly, with no stains, no traces left behind.

Yet even with the current government there had been a slight easing of paranoia, a willingness to tolerate some dissension from majority (i.e., the praetor's) opinion. More and more, senators spoke their minds and lived. Donatra began to feel hope. For though she was raised in the military—both her parents had reached the rank of commander—she was also raised to think freely, even if society required her to keep those thoughts to herself.

Her father, however, a severely handsome male with blazing intelligence and confidence, had one day overstepped his bounds and violated the very rule he had taught her. He had spoken in private with the praetor concerning the abuse of the native population of the Xanara system; the usual Romulan method of conquering and enslaving did not work with these particular creatures, who valued meaningful existence more than they valued existence itself. Mass suicide was the general result—and there was no profit to Romulus from suicide. Was it possible, her father had suggested, that the Empire adapt its approach to allow the Xanarans their meaning while still profiting from an alliance?

He had offered a solution; the praetor had thanked him. And that night, he joined the ranks of the disappeared. Neither Donatra nor her mother ever spoke of it; they knew their encounters were under the Empire's watchful eye. Their grieving was private and separate. To protect her nine-year-old daughter, Donatra's mother immediately surrendered her to the care of the military academy, under the auspices of the unquestionably loyal, unquestionably powerful family friend, Commander Suran.

Suran was a generation older than Donatra's parents, a favorite of the then-current praetor's, and the perfect candidate to foster the girl. Such arrangements were quite common, either to allow a child special privilege, or to allow her escape from political stigma; in Suran's case, his status allowed

Donatra both. She was required to cut off all ties to her mother, and Suran became her parent, mentor, instructor.

He fulfilled all roles admirably, leaving Donatra deeply grateful and a full commander at an early age. She had been fearful at first that Suran had made his choice because of her beauty, something her mother had warned was possible, and that when she came of age, more than loyalty might be expected of her. Yet Suran remained honorable, maintaining the position of mentor, nothing more. Donatra was willing to die for him.

Now, Commander Suran walked by her side as they made their way down the shadowy corridor, past the flickering braziers, toward the Chamber itself. His hair had long ago turned to iron, but his eyebrows were pure white, and the glowing coals painted them pale red.

Suran was speaking.

"The fleet commanders are nervous," he said. "They've agreed to remain at their given coordinates and await their orders. But they're anxious to know what's going on here."

Donatra herself was somewhat nervous, though she would never permit such weakness to show. She was required, out of loyalty, to follow Suran into the Chamber; but she tried to suppress imagining any images of what had recently transpired there. "I don't blame them," she said tersely. "We can't keep them in the dark forever."

Words came from the unseen void ahead.

"But in darkness, there is strength." The voice was deep, and gentle in a way that made Donatra's flesh crawl.

A creature stepped forward from the shadows. Compared to the Romulans, he was unsettlingly tall and powerful, with a long, gaunt face and skin whiter than the ash from the burning brazier coals. This was the viceroy, Shinzon's second-in-command—and he was the first Reman Donatra had ever seen. She understood at once why Romulan myth had turned them into beings that peopled children's nightmares: the viceroy's features were skeletal, his eyes deep, shadowed sockets, his huge, elongated build reminiscent of a legendary nocturnal monster that supposedly stole children from beds and ate them, limb by limb, cracking the bones with his powerful jaws. He had the teeth to do so, certainly—sharp fangs with elongated incisors, and his pale, semitransparent ears were pointed like a Romulan's, but twice as large and standing away from his gaunt cheeks.

Donatra allowed herself no reaction, merely gazed up at him with an expression calculated to convey fearlessness.

"Don't you agree?" the viceroy continued, with a small, lethal smile, then turned, and led them onward.

Donatra had been inside the Senate Chamber several times in her life; now it was so transformed as to be unrecognizable. Only hours before, this chamber had been filled with light and sound and the warm bodies of some hundred living senators. Now it was eerily deserted, shrouded in darkness eased only by the light from crude Reman torches.

They illuminated the great wall bearing the crest of the bird of prey, Romulus and Remus in its talons; the floor beneath had metamorphosed into the blackness of space, dotted with stars.

"Consider it . . . The great symbol of the Empire," a voice intoned. This was not the viceroy speaking; the voice was neither deep nor gentle, but resonant and instantly arresting. This was the voice of power.

Donatra scanned the darkness, and as her eyes adjusted, she saw the voice's owner standing beneath the great crest: an adult male human, handsome and young by Earth standards, his scalp hairless, his complexion white as a Reman's—so phosphorescent pale that Donatra wondered how she had failed to notice him immediately. He wore a Reman military uniform rendered monochrome by the dimness, and his bearing, as he stood upon space and the stars, was straight and solid, that of a natural leader.

Though she had never met him, she knew him at once to be Shinzon, the human raised by Remans.

"But the bird of prey holds *two* planets," Shinzon continued. "Romulus *and* Remus. Their destinies conjoined. Yet for generations one of those planets has been without a voice . . . We will be silent no longer."

As Donatra's eyes continued to adjust, she noticed others in the huge chamber: Senator Tal'Aura, she who had so recently detonated the weapon that changed Romulan history; two commanders who had tried, and failed, to convince the praetor to ally himself with Shinzon; and, at strategic posts, a contingent of armed Reman soldiers—pale ghosts standing guard in the night.

Shinzon at last ceased his oratory and took note of the two recent arrivals. "Join us, Commanders," he said pleasantly. He addressed himself then to Suran alone. "Now what's the disposition of the fleet?"

"They're holding position," Suran replied, his demeanor one of great respect.

"And?" Shinzon lifted his eyebrows, so thin they were almost invisible. To Donatra's Romulan eyes, humans had always appeared bland and browless, as if their foreheads and ears had never completely formed. Odd and unfinished, she thought, but the lack of drama in Shinzon's appearance was more than compensated for by the intensity in his stance, his voice, his gaze. He was not unhandsome.

Suran bowed his head; for some reason, it troubled Donatra to see her beloved mentor humbling himself before an outworlder—but she maintained a neutral expression. "They will obey, Praetor," Suran replied.

"It's imperative we retain their allegiance or our great mission will be strangled before it can truly draw breath." Shinzon's tone held a warning.

Donatra spoke up, ignoring Suran's sidewise glance. "They support your intentions, sir. But they require evidence of your . . . shall we say . . . *sincerity*."

Perhaps it was foolish of her, speaking to the legendary Shinzon this way, at his moment of triumph. She risked not only her own life but something of far greater value to her— Suran's approval. But she had to know: Was this Shinzon merely another praetor who could tolerate no brave minds speaking the truth? Would he assassinate her, like a coward, so that she joined her father as one of the disappeared? Or was he strong enough to listen?

Shinzon fixed his gaze upon hers; she held it, unafraid. Unlike Suran, she would not bow her head.

For less than an instant, less than the time it takes a Romulan heart to squeeze out a single rapid beat, Donatra thought she saw madness in his eyes; she thought he would call to one of his pale ghosts and have her blood spilled there, on the starlit floor.

The instant passed so swiftly she could not be sure what she had seen; Shinzon's gaze turned benevolent; he smiled genuinely, without scorn or malice.

"And they'll have it." He folded his hands behind his back and began to pace away from her, across the star chart. To Commander Suran, he said: "Tell the fleet that the days of negotiation and diplomacy are over. The 'mighty' Federation will fall before us. As I promised you." He paused; beneath his feet lay the area of space designated centuries before as the Neutral Zone between the Romulan Empire and the United Federation of Planets.

"The time we have dreamed of is at hand," Shinzon, once again the dramatic orator, promised. "The time . . . of *conquest.*"

With a single, deliberate step, he crossed over the line into the area of space marked with the Federation symbol. He glanced down and with satisfaction said, as if to himself: "Cut off the dragon's head and it cannot strike back."

For a moment, he gazed at his goal silently; again, something in his eyes troubled Donatra.

"And how many warbirds will you need to 'slay the dragon'?" she asked.

He returned from his reverie at once and smiled up at her—again, the benevolent leader. "You don't approve of my oratory."

Donatra refused to be swayed by his attempt to win her through self-deprecation. She did not change her expression or tone. "Pretty words are of little use in battle."

He took no offense, but the ingratiating smile faded; as he spoke, his tone hardened. "Wars are fought and civilizations made and lost over pretty words like 'glory' and 'honor' and 'freedom.' You miss so much of life, Commander, looking only at battle maps and fleet protocols . . ." He paused, glanced down at the stars beneath him, then told both Donatra and Suran: "In any event, I will need no warbirds."

Donatra's lips parted with surprise; and Suran, immovable Suran who had kept his poise through the pronouncements of three Romulan praetors and innumerable battles, stared wide-eyed at his new leader.

"Praetor," Suran countered with disbelief, "You have the whole fleet at your disposal. They supported the coup, they'll follow you."

Was that not, after all, the point of Shinzon's courtship of the Romulan military? Donatra wondered. If he did not need them, why recruit them?

"The *Scimitar* will serve my needs," Shinzon said shortly.

The *Scimitar,* his own vessel: one ship against the entire Federation. *Surely*, Donatra thought, *this one is mad.*

"I came this far alone," Shinzon said, then glanced at his Reman warriors and corrected himself. "*We* came this far alone. We require no assistance from the fleet. Now leave me." He turned about to direct his last words to all Romulans in the room. Along with Senator Tal'Aura, the four commanders strode from the room, each one mystified.

There was something entirely wrong with the scenario, Donatra decided, and something most definitely wrong with the new praetor. As a Romulan, she could understand the desire for war, for glory, for power. She could understand a new praetor demanding the support of the fleet, demanding warbirds.

But the sense she had gotten when first seeing Shinzon, that something was missing—that sense had been caused by more than just his human appearance. Something deeper, something within was missing from him, creating a void that power and the entire Romulan fleet and all its warbirds could not fill. And that troubled her most of all . . .

Once the Romulans left the chamber, Shinzon sighed deeply and consciously let the muscles of his abdomen and solar plexus relax. Hatred made him tense; and there was none he hated more than the Romulans, despite his presentation of himself as their praetor and ally. He could not hear a Romulan voice, see a Romulan face without feeling the phaser lash against the skin of his back. In time, he would repay their convenient loyalty with justice: Let them serve the Remans, as the Remans had once served them.

Until then, he would smile at Suran and Donatra, at Senator Tal'Aura, and thank them for their cooperation.

And he would be grateful that now, at this very moment, his Reman friends were enjoying their first taste of justice, standing at last in the Senate Chamber, where representation had so long been denied them. He looked, smiling, at his viceroy—gentlest and truest of friends—and knew that beneath the impassive Reman demeanor, there was joy.

For until this Romulan night, to be Reman was to live a life of unending labor and cruel punishment, a life with no physical comfort. To be Reman was to be born at one of the Empire's breeding facilities on the planet, where the hardiest of males were mated under coercion to the hardiest of females, then sent to the dilithium mines as soon as one could stand.

(Certainly, the Romulans had the technology for cloning, or for in vitro births—but the more brutal way used for centuries stayed in place, to strip the Remans of all dignity, to remind them of the Empire's power over even the most sacred of personal rights.) *Father, mother, sister, brother:* These were terms used fondly, when relaying tales of earlier times, when clans dwelled together. To be Reman was never to know one's family, but to be property of the Romulan government. To be Reman was to go hungry. Food was scarce and often putrid, save for the burrowing rodents one managed to catch in the mines (so long as they could be devoured quickly, before a guard happened by and administered a phaser lash). To be Reman was to be considered an unintelligent beast from a backward culture.

But Shinzon knew the deep and abiding intelligence of his former fellow slaves. He had not always known; years before, he had been thrown into the dark mine pits, a cowering boy of little significance. The Romulan guard who hurled him from the lift had laughed at him, saying: *Mind those sharp Reman teeth; they'll make quick work of a puny human*, and he had believed them.

That was before the very first Reman he had ever seen, a fanged ghoul, had emerged from the shadows, terrifying the lad, and reached a clawlike hand toward the human's.

The nameless boy expected the monster to rip his limb off; instead, the Reman gently took his hand.

The human had felt many sensations at once, sensations that touched his mind, his emotions. Without words, without detectable telepathy, the Reman imparted a great deal of knowledge about himself, about his lightless world.

His name was Vkruk. He had worked his entire life, to his earliest memory, in this dilithium mine. Life was suffering at the hands of the Empire's guards, angry men who had been demoted from military service to prison work on a world that the Romulans nicknamed Black Hell. Yet through courage and loyalty to fellow Remans, purpose, even beauty, could be found in the midst of such a wretched existence. No Reman ever betrayed or hurt another; any Reman would risk his life for another, and gladly die in his brother's place. Yet their ferocity toward those who hurt their brothers was renowned. These beliefs, and a dogged hope that the time of clans would return, constituted their religion.

You are a noble people, the human had said, without speaking, and in that instant, he resolved to bring the time of clans to pass, if he had to die achieving it. For he himself had been denied a family by the Romulan Empire; he had no roots, but he would plant them in Remus's dark soil.

It was then Vkruk gave him his name: Shinzon. In Reman, the word meant *liberator*, and at the same time that the human thought to himself that he would free Remus's slaves, Vkruk conveyed simultaneously that the human *was* the liberator, Shinzon, predicted by Reman legend—a Reman, yet not a Reman, who would end the suffering and unite the clans.

Shinzon embraced the name, thinking: *And I name you my viceroy.*

Without speech, the viceroy understood the implications of the name, and smiled.

• • •

Now the time of the liberation of clans had finally come; even now, Reman soldiers were freeing their women from the breeding houses, while others were preparing for the battle to come against the Federation. But so loyal were the Remans that they would not let their leader, their Shinzon, achieve freedom only for them. The viceroy had sensed Shinzon's deepest wish, to claim the homeworld from which he was stolen, to find the one that was all to him: father, brother, Self. With a touch, he had explained to his human friend the soldiers' collective agreement that Shinzon's desire must first be fulfilled.

Shinzon himself could not deny it: his yearning to find the one who was his source had become as overwhelming as his desire to liberate his fellow slaves. Now that the latter had been fulfilled, he was desperate for the former.

That was before they had found the Romulan medical records on the human; before they discovered the facts that compelled him to find his other Self. Suddenly, the need to find the one became overwhelming, mandatory.

So Shinzon looked to his viceroy and asked, "Are we prepared?"

"Yes, Praetor."

For a moment, Shinzon was too overwhelmed to reply; he bowed his head. At last, he whispered, "So many years for this moment . . ." He raised his face and smiled at the viceroy. "Bring him to me."

On the *Enterprise* bridge, Deanna Troi was having difficulty coaxing a recalcitrant Klingon into a new experience . . . and up to that point, Will was remaining silent while Data regarded the exchange with curiosity.

"I won't do it," Worf grumbled.

"It's *tradition*, Worf," Troi said, managing to keep most of the exasperation from her tone. While she had thoroughly enjoyed her Alaskan wedding and felt a deep, solid happiness, on the surface she still suffered from the frayed nerves involved with arranging nuptials—even if Will had done half the work. *One down,* Will had said with deep relief the instant they were alone after the wedding, and she had sighed along with him, then reminded him: *And one to go.* He'd rolled his eyes, and she'd made a comment about the wisdom of eloping.

Oh, no, Will had said, with mock terror. *I can deal with ticking off my father, but Lwaxana . . .*

She'd laughed then, and relaxed about the whole thing. But a faint wave of preceremony anxiety came over her now as Worf said sternly, "A warrior does not appear without his clothing. It leaves him . . . vulnerable."

"I don't think we're going to see much combat on Betazed," Will said, his expression deadpan.

Deanna looked gratefully over at him, and felt the tension in her abdomen suddenly release. Will was right, of course . . . the only way to approach all the planning, pomp, and circumstance was with humor. She quit worrying about what others would think of a guest in clothing and instead said with a straight face, "Don't be too sure . . . Mother will be there."

Worf groaned aloud just as the captain emerged from the ready room and took the conn from Will.

"I won't do it," the Klingon proclaimed loudly.

"Won't do what, Mister Worf?" Picard asked.

"Captain . . ." the Klingon began, his expression one of distaste mixed with embarrassment. "I think it is inappropriate for a Starfleet officer to appear . . ." He anguished for a long time over the word before finally saying, "naked."

Picard's expression brightened at once, and his tone became exceptionally cheerful. "Come now, a big, strapping fellow like you? What are you afraid of?"

Before she restrained herself, Deanna laughed aloud. She fully expected the Klingon to turn sharply with some retort, but instead Worf's attention was diverted to the readout on his console.

"I'm picking up an unusual electromagnetic signature from the Kolarin system."

"What sort of signature?" Picard leaned forward in his chair.

Worf glanced up from his readout, then gazed over at Data. "Positronic."

Later on the bridge, at the engineering station, Picard listened along with Data and Riker as Geordi La Forge made his report. On the console was readout of a starchart pinpointing a sun and its planets.

"It's very faint," Geordi explained, "but I've isolated it to the third planet in the Kolarin system."

"What do we know about the planet?" Picard asked.

"Uncharted. We'll have to get closer for a more detailed scan."

Picard turned his head to face Data. "Theories?"

Data replied at once. "Since positronic signatures have

only been known to emanate from androids such as myself, it is logical to theorize that there is an android such as myself on Kolarus Three."

Geordi's forehead wrinkled. "How many of you did Dr. Soong make?"

"I thought only myself and my brother Lore."

Riker studied the star chart. "Diverting to the Kolarin system takes us awfully close to the Romulan Neutral Zone."

Picard followed his second-in-command's gaze. "Still well on our side . . ." He glanced over at Data. He knew how deeply the android wanted to find others like himself; and the diversion to Kolarus III would take minimal time . . . "I think it's worth a look," he said finally. "Don't worry, Number One, we'll get you to Betazed with time to spare."

Riker grinned. "Thank you, sir."

Picard raised his voice, specifically for the benefit of Worf. "Where we will *all* honor the Betazoid traditions . . . Now, if you'll excuse me, I'll be in the gym."

He left.

Riker addressed the helm officer at once. "Mister Branson, set course for the Kolarin system. Warp five—" He broke off, realizing that Deanna was making him the recipient of one of her most dangerous gazes. "Warp seven."

"Plotted and laid in, sir," Branson said, and Deanna's expression warmed at once.

"Engage," Riker said.

Meanwhile, at the engineering station, Geordi and Data continued to study the display.

"What do you think, Data, a long-lost relative?" La Forge asked softly.

The android did not reply, merely cocked his head and continued to gaze curiously at the readout, as if by looking at it long enough, he would uncover the mystery . . .

Chapter 3

The bridge's main viewscreen showed Kolarus III, a mottle of white, green, and blue as it lazily orbited its sun. In the distance, space flickered and sparked with a violent ion storm. Picard watched the tableau before him and wondered if he had come here as a way of delaying Will and Deanna's inevitable departure—then dismissed the thought at once. Anyone on the *Enterprise* would have taken the extra time for a chance at finding another Data.

From the engineering station, La Forge called out, "I read six distinct positronic signatures, spread out over a few kilometers on the surface."

Picard tried to imagine six Datas all together at once and failed. "What do we know about the population?"

"Isolated pockets of humanoids," Data replied from his console. "It appears to be a prewarp civilization at an early stage of industrial development."

Geordi looked up from his station and shook his head.

"Captain, I don't recommend transporting; that ion storm doesn't look very neighborly. It could head this way without much warning."

"Understood." Picard rose. "Data, Worf, you're with me."

The two officers began to follow their captain toward the turbolift.

Riker stood at once. "Captain," he protested, "I hope I don't have to remind you—"

Picard's tone lightened. "I appreciate your concern, Number One, but I've been itching to try out the *Argo*."

Riker grinned. "I'll bet."

Picard smiled back. "Captain's prerogative, Will. There's no foreseeable danger . . . and your wife would never forgive me if anything happened to you . . ." He stepped into the turbolift with Data and Worf, and while the doors were still open, announced loudly, "You have the bridge, Mister Troi."

The doors slid shut. Picard's smile turned smug; he only wished he could have witnessed the reaction.

The *Argo* turned out to be a fine piece of engineering, landing smoothly on Kolarus III's rugged surface—but the large shuttle, designed for ship-to-planet transport, was not the actual vehicle Picard was most interested in testing. As the away team waited for the cargo bay doors to open, the captain smiled faintly to himself as he sat in the pilot's seat of Starfleet's newest land vehicle; Data sat beside him, in the copilot's chair, with Worf sitting in the rear.

The vehicle was a four-wheeled affair, an open structure of curving silver metal bars—two bars arching from just behind the two passenger seats to form a curved rollbar roof, and extending forward to just past the front engine. In the rear was the tall, caged structure where a third party could hold on and, if necessary, fire the weaponry hidden in the flooring.

At last the shuttle doors slid open, revealing a desert landscape: bleached sandy soil, boulders and sparse vegetation beneath a ruthless sun. The *Argo* had landed in center of a valley; in the distance, clay-colored mountains and canyons were obscured from time to time by dark, roiling heat waves—how much distance, it was impossible for Picard to judge; he knew deserts to be deceptive in that manner. He breathed in. The air was hot, scented with the herbaceous smell of dried brush, but the vehicle kept a comfortable cushion of coolness around the passengers.

With a sense of playfulness, Picard accelerated the land vehicle forward—why not, after all, enjoy the moment, since it would all too soon end? To his delight, the vehicle roared out of the shuttle with a gratifying surge of power and speed. Just as suddenly, he braked, causing Data and Worf to lurch forward in their seats and raising a fine cloud of dust.

Data took advantage of his forward momentum to press the controls on the dashboard panel; behind them, the doors to the *Argo*'s cargo bay slid shut. The android then glanced down at his tricorder and reported: "The closest signature is two kilometers to the west . . ." He inclined his head. "That direction, sir."

"Thank you, Data," Picard replied, then allowed himself a slightly wicked smile. "Let's see what she can do."

And he accelerated the vehicle to breakneck speed, enjoying the purely visceral sensation of contact with the ground, the feel of each rock and dip on the planet surface, the vibration of the machine itself. Even the rush of air against his exposed skin was exhilarating. His grin widened; he turned to Data and Worf to comment on the experience, but it was clear the other two failed to share in their captain's enjoyment. Data clung desperately to the dashboard, while Worf, in the rear, was grasping the rollbar so tightly his knuckles had paled by several shades.

The android spoke before Picard could. "I will always be baffled by the human predilection for piloting vehicles at unsafe velocities."

Picard smiled to himself and accelerated a bit more.

Data continued to monitor with the tricorder and at last said, "Over that rise, sir . . . half a kilometer."

Half a kilometer came all too soon, in Picard's estimation; nevertheless, he stopped where Data indicated, and the three climbed out of the vehicle. It was, Picard thought, like climbing into a furnace: Without clouds, without a speck of moisture in the air, the sun's rays shone down with especial ferocity. It reminded him of Vulcan, and he admired the local populace's ability to function.

Data's focus on the tricorder became intense. "The radiant EM field is interfering with my tricorder, but we are within a few meters of the signal."

Picard brushed fast-gathering beads of sweat from his brow and moved about slowly, scanning the rocks and flat, baked earth for signs of . . . circuitry? An android creator? Whatever was here could scarcely be the work of the inhabitants. Data and Worf followed suit, moving slowly off in different directions, searching.

An abrupt snaking sound, something lashing swiftly through the sand. Picard whirled to catch a glimpse of what he first thought was some sort of reptilian creature, a cobra, perhaps, seizing Worf's ankle, at the same moment that the Klingon jumped, astonished.

But the item that Worf pulled with distaste from his ankle was far from reptilian: it was an arm. A sentient arm, with a hand that flailed about in the air, seeking purchase, as Worf held it. The sight was somehow grisly; even the Klingon shuddered.

Data, however, seemed pleased as he immediately scanned it. "It appears to be a robotic arm."

"Very astute," Worf grumbled.

"Why is it moving?" Picard asked.

Data's tone was decidedly cheerful for one who felt no emotion. "Like me, it has been designed with modular power sources."

Picard headed for the land vehicle and gestured at the rear cargo area; Worf at once set the arm there and the three retook their seats. Data glanced down at his tricorder again.

"The next signature is one kilometer to the south."

Once again, Picard allowed himself the pleasure of hurtling over the desert soil at top speed. Within the space of an hour, at different areas in the Kolaran desert, the trio retrieved a second arm, two legs, and a torso—the latter undressed, of dark, unpolished metal. Picard felt an odd sense of invading the unassembled parts' privacy, as if he had caught Data undressed without asking permission.

Now they had all but one component of a positronic android.

Standing in the rear of the vehicle, Worf glanced uneasily down at the cargo area, where the disassembled body parts writhed. Meanwhile, Data made a final scan with his tricorder.

"The final signature is approximately one hundred meters to the north, sir."

The three set off once more; Picard slowed, then stopped at precisely one hundred meters. For a moment, he saw nothing but dark undulating waves of heat rising from the soil and then his eye spotted something oval and pale gold against the coppery sand.

"It's . . . you," Worf said, astonished.

"The resemblance is . . . striking," Data said with android matter-of-factness.

Picard said nothing. He had expected to find positronic circuitry at least, an android at most. But he had not been quite prepared to find another Data.

They left the vehicle and went toward the disembodied head. Data reached it first and leaned down to look: It had apparently lain in the desert some time. Its hair was covered with a fine layer of dust, its forehead, cheeks, and chin smudged with dirt.

At once the head's eyes popped open. It gazed upon Data with a dullness Picard had not expected, then asked: "Why am I looking at me?"

"You are not looking at yourself," Data said. "You are looking at me."

The head moved with the familiar, slightly jerky movements of its double to look up at the Klingon. "You do not look like me," it said.

"No," Worf replied, sounding pleased about the matter.

Gently, Data said, "I would like to pick you up now. May I do that?"

The head offered no objection; instead, with the fleeting attention span of a four-year-old, it gazed up at Picard. "You have a pretty shirt."

"Thank you," the captain murmured, slightly taken aback.

Data carefully picked up the head, and the two identical faces studied each other. "Fascinating . . ." Data said. He held it in both arms, stretched a slight distance from him that he might better scrutinize it. The gesture and posture were so reminiscent of a scene from Shakespeare that Picard opened his mouth to recite, *Alas, poor Yorick . . .*

But his comments were interrupted by a loud explosion. Instinctively, Picard ducked and spun, realizing that a nearby boulder had just been reduced to rubble. A group of nomadic inhabitants were racing in crude desert terrain vehicles toward the trio; the explosion had been caused by the primitive plasma weapons fired by gunners on the roofs.

"Come on!" Picard shouted.

He and his officers leapt back into their vehicle; this time, Picard took even less care to ensure a smooth take off. As the aliens pursued, he turned to Data. "Shall we try some 'unsafe velocities'?" He pushed the accelerator all the way to maximum, throwing up clouds of dust. Behind him, Worf pressed the control that brought up the mounted phaser cannon; Picard heard him blast away at the aliens' vehicles, heard the crashes as some of them overturned.

Beside him, Data still cradled the head. It looked over at Picard with piercing ingenuousness and said, "You have a shiny head."

Data addressed it as a parent would a child. "This is not an appropriate time for a conversation."

"Why?" the head asked, and Picard suddenly remembered one aspect of children that always irritated him.

"Because the captain has to concentrate on piloting the vehicle," Data explained patiently.

"Why?"

Data took a breath to respond, but Picard had had enough. "Data!" he barked.

"Sorry, sir," the android said.

Despite the real-enough danger, Picard felt a thrill of true exhilaration as the land vehicle raced over the landscape at top speed, bouncing over rises in the terrain so that his stomach lurched with the momentary thrill of flying. He steered the vehicle in a serpentine pattern to avoid the constant fire, while Worf continued firing the cannon; soon, they were within sight of the *Argo*.

Which, unfortunately, was surrounded by a second contingent of aliens—close enough now for the captain to make out their features, a dark olive green which appeared to be sculpted from the very desert rock that surounded them.

"Mister Data," Picard began.

He needed say no more. The android understood at once and pressed the dashboard remote control that caused the *Argo*—much to the aliens' surprise—to lift off. As Data flew the *Argo* ahead of the land vehicle, the second group of aliens charged, firing their weapons at the away team.

At the same time, the first group of aliens pursued from the rear.

Sandwiched between bursts of plasma fire, the roar of primitive engines and the guttural shouts of humanoids that seemed constructed of piles of stones, Picard kept the land vehicle moving at a speed that left the three bouncing and breathless. His exhilaration had left him entirely, replaced now by a desperate focus on following the flying *Argo*. Although Data's remote maneuvering of the shuttlecraft was skillful, the constant plasma bursts and approaching aliens made it impossible for him to stop the craft long enough for the land vehicle to board. Worf kept overturning alien vehicles with fire from the phaser cannon, but more kept appearing from hiding places behind rocks, as if swarms were hidden in some secret grotto beneath the earth.

Picard was finally admitting to himself that he had taken too few precautions to protect his people from the inhabitants when he saw a way out: a natural rise in the terrain, perpendicular to *Argo*'s current trajectory. He glanced at it, then nodded to the android beside him. "Data."

Data followed the captain's gaze to the rise, and gave a swift nod to indicate he understood.

Picard spun the wheel hard, causing the land vehicle to veer sharply toward their new destination; Data leaned over the dashboard console, working with preternatural speed to position the *Argo* just beyond it, and open the shuttle's rear cargo bay doors.

Up the vehicle went, over the berm as if it were a ramp, and became airborne.

Picard did not permit himself to look down—for in midair, his peripheral vision made him uncomfortably aware that there was nothing at all past the berm except a very, very long way down. His makeshift ramp was, in fact, the edge of a high cliff.

He drew in his breath, held on tightly to the wheel, and heard Worf behind him emit a very small moan.

And then, in the next heartbeat, the wheels of the vehicle slammed down against the deck of the *Argo*'s cargo bay. Picard hit the brakes, which responded with a loud shriek that echoed off the bulkheads as the doors behind the away team closed.

Picard's pulse was still racing, but he could not help taking some childish glee in the fact that Worf and Data had not yet recovered from the wild ride. Wearing a deadpan expression, he climbed from the vehicle as if he had just been on an easy sightseeing tour, paused to wipe some dust from the hood, then headed for the main cabin—leaving Worf and Data still sitting, stunned and frozen, behind him.

In the engineering lab, Picard watched as Beverly and Riker studied the new, still-disassembled android while Data stood by like a family member waiting to hear a medical report. The android's parts were currently held in place by a framework that was designed by Geordi, who at the moment was scanning the torso.

Beverly was leaning forward to gaze at the android's head, which gazed blankly back at her.

"I think you have nicer eyes," she said to Data.

"Our eyes are identical, Doctor," Data replied.

It was quite true. Yet, at the same time, Beverly had a point: though Data's eyes were, in a way, ingenuous as his double's, there was something intangibly warmer about them. Recognition of the others, and his surroundings, perhaps; a gregariousness, a personality.

"Geordi?" Riker, standing next to Picard, asked for a report.

Geordi studied his readout. "Well, he seems to have the

same internal mechanics as Data, but not as much positronic development. The neural pathways aren't nearly as sophisticated." He stopped scanning and looked up at Riker and the captain. "I'd say he's . . . a prototype. Something Dr. Soong created before Data."

Data addressed the head politely. "Do you have a name, sir?"

The head blinked, then said, with the same childlike intonation it had always used, "I am the B-four."

"Be-fore," Picard echoed dryly. "Dr. Soong's penchant for whimsical names seems to have no end."

"Can you tell me how you came to be on the planet where we found you?"

"I do not know," B-4 replied.

"Do you remember anything of your life before you were on the planet?"

"No . . ." B-4's attention wandered to Riker's beard. "You have a fuzzy face."

Picard was glad, after all, that he had made the side journey to Kolarus III, for Data's sake; android or not, Data would regard the B-4 as long-lost family. The captain turned to Riker. "Keep me informed, Number One, and, please; put him back together." He headed out.

"Do you know who I am?" Data asked his double.

"You are me."

Data shook his head. "No. My name is Data. I am your brother."

In the crew lounge that evening, Deanna was enjoying dinner with Will and Worf. It had taken some coaxing on

Deanna's part, but she had finally gotten Worf less uncomfortable about shedding his uniform for the ceremony on Betazed. Now they were discussing the honeymoon—the one thing upon which both she and Will agreed made all the formalities worthwhile.

"And after the ceremony on Betazed," she said to Worf, "three entire weeks for our honeymoon." She had repeated the statement many times to many different people, but it still seemed like a dream; she hadn't had that much time off in years, much less taken a real vacation with the man she loved. She leaned against him.

Will grinned at the very thought of it, white teeth flashing beneath his dark mustache. "We're going sailing on the Opal Sea. We've booked an old-fashioned solar catamaran. Just us and the sun and the waves."

Worf listened with polite interest, then said, "It seems a very . . . soft honeymoon."

Deanna smiled to herself, amused; she had considered it romantic, but rather spartan. "It's meant to be relaxing."

The Klingon grunted. "A Klingon honeymoon begins with the Kholamar desert march where the couple bonds in endurance trials. If they survive the challenge, they move on to the Fire Caves of Fek'lhr to face the demons of Gre'thor."

"Well, that sounds relaxing, too," Riker quipped.

Worf, of course, took the statement at face value and seemed pleased. "It is . . . invigorating."

Deanna looked away, toward the lounge entry, distracted by the sight of Data leading B-4, as a parent might lead a child into a classroom on its first day of school.

"So they've got him up and running," Will remarked.

"He is a very . . . unusual android," Worf added. Deanna noted that this admission seemed to make the Klingon a bit uncomfortable, as if he were somehow being disloyal to Data.

Will smiled, always ready with the right words to put everyone at ease. "Runs in the family."

They watched as Data led the B-4 to a table, showed him how to sit, then sat across from him and instructed him in the use of a napkin. Through it all, the B-4 sat placidly; a true tabula rasa, Deanna thought, yet there was something very touching about the interaction between the two. And poignant: For though the B-4 was Data's double, he was slow and simple, no match for Data's curiosity and intelligence.

In his ready room, Picard stood at his replicator unit, mulling over the implications of a second android aboard the *Enterprise,* and said absently, "Tea. Earl Grey, hot."

He was just picking up the steaming cup when a comm signal chimed softly.

The voice was Riker's. "Captain, you have an alpha priority communication from Starfleet Command."

"Acknowledged." More than curious, Picard returned to his desk and set down the tea. He could only hope the news was not bad. Alpha priority was reserved for the most important of messages: an uprising on a Federation planet, a system-wide disaster, war . . . He activated the viewscreen.

Admiral Kathryn Janeway, former captain of the *Voyager,* looked hale and fit and completely comfortable in her new rank.

"Admiral Janeway." Picard smiled. "Good to see you." Clearly, the news she brought wasn't all bad; she returned his smile, and her arms were folded in a relaxed manner atop her desk.

"Jean-Luc," she said, in a tone laced with dry wit. "How'd you like a trip to Romulus?"

"With or without the rest of the fleet?" he countered. If things weren't bad, they were, at the very least, of grave import despite Janeway's apparent ease.

"A diplomatic mission." Her next words left Picard astounded. "We've been invited, believe it or not. Seems there's been some kind of internal political shakeup. The new praetor, someone called Shinzon, has requested a Federation envoy."

"New praetor?"

"There's more," Janeway said. "He's *Reman* . . ."

This time, Picard could not keep his lips from parting in surprise.

Janeway took note of it and added, "Believe me, we don't understand it either. You're the closest ship, so I want you to go and hear what he has to say. Get the lay of the land. If the Empire becomes unstable, it could mean trouble for the entire quadrant."

Picard focused himself. "Understood."

"We're sending you all the intelligence we have, but it's not much . . . I don't need to tell you to watch your back, Jean-Luc."

"Not with the Romulans."

Janeway gave a wry little smile. "The Son'a, the Borg, the Romulans . . . You seem to get all the easy assignments."

"Just lucky, Admiral."

"Let's hope that luck holds," Janeway said. "Janeway out."

• • •

On the bridge, Picard took the conn from Riker and ordered the helm, "Lay in a new course. Take us to Romulus. Warp eight."

Every crewmember turned to look at him with shock.

"Aye, aye, sir," the helm officer said at last. "Course plotted and laid in."

Beside him, Riker asked in disbelief, "Romulus?" It was clearly *not* the course he'd expected.

"I'm afraid the Opal Sea will have to wait, Number One . . . Engage."

And the *Enterprise* leapt into warp, hurtling toward the Neutral Zone.

In the *Enterprise* observation lounge, Picard sat and listened as Data conducted a briefing for the senior officers. The captain was none too pleased about having to postpone Deanna and Riker's departure, much less dragging them into a potentially dangerous situation, but such was the life of a Starfleet officer, and there could be no delay in obeying an alpha priority order from headquarters.

The monitors displayed images of Romulus and Remus in orbit around their sun.

"As you can see," Data was saying, "one side of Remus always faces the sun. Due to the extreme temperatures on that half of their world, the Remans live on the dark side of the planet. Almost nothing is known about the Reman homeworld, although intelligence scans have proven the existence of dilithium mining and heavy weapons construction. The Remans themselves are considered an undesirable caste in the hierarchy of the Empire."

"But they also have the reputation of being formidable warriors," Riker pointed out. "In the Dominion War, Reman forces were used as assault troops in the most violent encounters."

"Cannon fodder," Picard said grimly.

Geordi shook his head. "Then how did a Reman get to be praetor? I don't get it."

"We have to assume he had Romulan collaborators," Riker said.

Picard turned to him. "A coup d'etat?"

Will nodded. "The praetor's power has always been the Romulan fleet. They must be behind him."

Picard considered this carefully, then looked to Data. "What have you learned about Shinzon?"

The viewscreens went blank; apparently, there were no images of the new praetor.

"Starfleet intelligence was only able to provide a partial account of his military record," Data said. "We can infer he is relatively young and a capable commander. He fought seventeen major engagements in the war. All successful. Beyond that, we know nothing."

"Well," Picard said. "It seems we're truly sailing into the unknown. Keep at it. Anything you can give me would be appreciated. Dismissed."

Given the surprise and import of the mission, the officers left in solemn silence; only Worf remained behind.

"Sir," the Klingon said respectfully. "I recommend we raise shields and go to Red Alert."

"Not quite yet, Commander."

Worf's gaze took on more than its usual intensity. "Permission to speak freely, sir . . ."

Picard nodded.

"I know the Romulans, and I don't trust them," Worf continued. "They live only for conquest. They are a people *without honor.* We are alone, well inside their territory. I recommend extreme caution."

Picard sympathized; but he also knew the violent images that fueled the commander's words: images of bloodied flesh, of murdered innocents. Of Worf's parents; of Khitomer.

"For better or worse," the captain said, "we're here on a diplomatic mission. I have to proceed under Federation protocols. But at the first sign of trouble, you can be assured, those protocols will no longer apply."

Worf's broad shoulders lowered, ever so slightly, as he released a breath, but the intensity in his eyes did not fade. "Thank you, sir."

In the engineering lab, Geordi La Forge had his hands full with two androids. At the moment, Data and the B-4 sat side by side, the circuitry in the heads connected by a series of conduits Geordi had constructed. Now, La Forge stood over his console, monitoring the exchange between the two.

In a way, the engineer had been glad for the distracting side trip that culminated in the discovery of the B-4: It allowed everyone the chance to work together again, to delay the departure of Riker and Troi and Dr. Crusher.

But there was something wrong with taking a strange android and trying to confer all of Data's unique abilities on it; and before Geordi realized he was thinking aloud, he muttered, "I can't believe the captain went along with a memory download."

Both androids were fully conscious during the procedure,

and Data was swift to respond. Emotionless or not, he clearly yearned for someone exactly like himself, someone who could understand him precisely. Had Data been wearing the emotion chip, Geordi decided, his next words would bear a defensive tone.

"Captain Picard agrees that the B-four was probably designed with the same self-actualization parameters as myself. If my memory engrams are successfully integrated into his positronic matrix, he should have all my abilities."

"He'd have all your memories, too," Geordi countered. "You comfortable with that?"

"I feel nothing, Geordi," Data replied. "It is my belief that with my memory engrams, he will be able to function as a more complete individual."

"An individual more like you, you mean."

"Yes." Data's tone was entirely matter-of-fact, free of the distress a human would feel at such a notion.

Geordi persisted; why did Data fail to see that he was a special individual, that creating an exact duplicate of himself diminished him? "Maybe he's not supposed to be like you. Maybe he's supposed to be just like he is."

"That might be so," Data agreed impassively. "But I believe he should be given the opportunity to explore his potential."

Geordi sighed as he eyed the console readout. "Okay. We're done."

He moved over to the androids and carefully removed the conduits connecting their positronic circuitry; carefully, he closed the panel in Data's head.

Data immediately addressed his double. "Do you know where you are?" The eagerness in his tone was unmistakable.

Both Geordi and his friend waited with anticipation as the B-4 paused to look at its surroundings. At last, it said, "I am in a room with lights."

"Can you remember our father?" Data asked.

The B-4's reply came faster this time. "No."

"Do you know my name?" Geordi asked.

The B-4 cocked its head, considering. "You have a soft voice."

Even though he disagreed with the idea of creating another Data, Geordi felt disappointment on behalf of his friend. Gently, he said, "Data, he's assimilating a lot of programming. We just don't know if his matrix will be able to adapt. Or if he'll be able to retain anything . . . We should give him some time."

As the engineer spoke, Data became fascinated by additional circuitry in the B-4's neck . . . circuitry which his more sophisticated counterpart did not share. Geordi ran a handheld scanner over it.

"It seems to be a redundant memory port. Maybe it's for provisional memory storage in case his neural pathways overload."

Data nodded. "Dr. Soong must have found it unnecessary in later versions."

"It's possible the extra memory port is interfering with the engram processing," Geordi said encouragingly. "Mind if I keep him here and run some diagnostics?"

"No, I don't mind," Data said. But he turned and looked at the B-4 with an expression so wistful, so crestfallen that Geordi felt sorry for him. At once, the engineer understood how difficult the loss of the emotion chip must have been for his friend; when the Borg queen had captured Data, she had so overloaded him with sensory and emotional input that the delicate chip had been destroyed. Although Geordi had tried to duplicate the chip for Data, his attempts had been unsuccessful; now he realized that here was something he could give to his friend to make up for Data's loss.

"Don't give up hope, Data," he said, then immediately corrected himself. "I know, I know, you're not capable of hope." *Then why,* he asked himself, *does Data look so sad? Am I projecting emotion onto him?*

"I am not," Data replied—but he continued looking at the B-4 with the same touching expression. At last, he stood.

The B-4 stood with him, as if linked by an invisible bond.

"No," Data said, mentor to student—or was it parent to child? "Remain with Commander La Forge. He is going to try to make you well."

Obediently, the B-4 sat while Data moved toward the exit. Geordi watched him go. And he realized, with a pang of guilt, that perhaps some of his reluctance to create a second Data was due to his unwillingness to lose the friendship of the first.

• • •

Captain's Log. Stardate 56844.9. The Enterprise *has arrived at Romulus and is waiting at the designated coordinates. All our hails have gone unanswered. We've been waiting for seventeen hours.*

On the main viewscreen, the great planet Romulus rotated slowly on its axis; in the distance, the blindingly bright half of Remus reflected the Romulan sun.

Picard sat quietly, aware of the tension that saturated the bridge. It was his job, as captain, to set an example for the crew—and so he maintained as relaxed a posture as possible, reminding everyone that they had arrived and were now merely waiting to fulfill their mission. Shinzon apparently wanted them nervous, and Picard was damned if he was going to give the new praetor what he wanted.

Even so, the captain had to monitor his own breath to keep it slow and steady, and remind himself to keep his belly relaxed.

At tactical, Worf broke the silence by stretching his neck: A small explosion resulted as the bones adjusted, causing Deanna Troi to jump slightly.

Will Riker could hold his tongue no more. "Why don't they answer our hails?"

"It's an old psychological strategy, Number One," Picard answered calmly. "To put him in a position of dominance and make us uneasy."

"It's working," Riker admitted grudgingly.

"Counselor?" Picard swiveled toward Troi, who had composed herself quite admirably; her shining black eyes seemed to pierce beyond what the viewscreen revealed.

"They're out there, sir." Her tone was one of utter certainty.

Picard rose and walked toward the viewscreen to gaze at Romulus below, and the blackness of space between them. Shinzon, he instinctively knew, even without Troi's confirmation, was closer than any of them could see.

Behind him, Worf urged, "Sir, I recommend we raise shields."

"Not yet, Mister Worf," Picard said slowly, without taking his gaze from the screen.

"Captain," Riker said, with not-entirely-veiled frustration, "with all due respect to diplomatic protocols—the Federation Council's not sitting out here, we are."

Picard turned toward him. "Patience . . . Diplomacy is a very exacting occupation. We can wait."

"Captain," Data said from the helm. There was no tension, no urgency in his tone as there had been in the others'. Yet the word electrified Picard; he turned at once back to the screen.

There, the fabric of space wavered, shimmering like heat waves that resolved themselves into the image of a magnificent Reman warbird—so close that it blocked all view of the planets beyond it, so close it more than filled the *Enterprise* viewscreen.

Picard drew in a silent breath. Riker rose from his chair, murmuring, "My God . . ."

The ship was massive, easily twice the size of the *Enterprise*. Its basic design was that of a Romulan warbird combined with unique weaponry and styling.

"Raising shields," Worf called.

"No," Picard commanded.

"Captain—!"

Picard's tone allowed no argument. "Tactical analysis, Mister Worf."

Worf directed his attention to his display. "Fifty-two disruptor banks, twenty-seven photon torpedo bays, primary and secondary phased shields."

"She's not out for a pleasure cruise," Riker said.

The captain's expression grew grim. "She's a predator."

"We're being hailed," Worf reported.

"On screen."

An image coalesced before them: that of a Reman bridge, dimly lit and elegantly spare, free of the mechanical clutter of a Federation ship. Even the being who addressed them stood rather than sat; in one hand he grasped a scepter.

"*Enterprise,*" he said, in a voice deep and guttural; his elongated, unsettlingly sharp fangs affected his articulation of certain consonants. "We are the Reman *Warbird Scimitar.*"

Picard had seen the images of Reman soldiers; he had been briefed on what to expect. Yet the sight of a living, breathing Reman still conjured up unpleasant images. A childhood memory returned to him at once: he and his brother had, for fun, looked at some ancient twentieth-century "movies," and had laughed aloud at a particular one intended to inspire horror— that of the blood-sucking Nosferatu, a pale, fanged creature with claws for hands, who had, at the end of the movie, been burned to death by the sun.

Picard stared at the Reman; he did not laugh now. As he adjusted to the sight and attempted to banish his prejudices, he studied the Reman's features more objectively. Perhaps they were initially frightening to humans because they seemed made not of skin, but entirely of sculpted bone, some prominent, some deeply shadowed; and perhaps because the huge domed forehead, combined with outswept, pointed ears, bridgeless nose, and prominent, fanged lower jaw was strongly reminiscent of the features of the Terran bat.

It did not help matters that they were famed as the galaxy's most fearsome warriors. But they clearly also had a refined sense of aesthetics; despite the dimness, Picard noted that the gleaming breastplate and sleeves of the Reman's uniform were shot through with hints of aubergine, that the console before him cast a handsome blue-green glow. Behind him, an upper deck glinted bronze.

"Praetor Shinzon," the captain said, in his most cordial diplomat's voice, "I'm pleased to—"

"I am not Shinzon," the Reman said. "I am his viceroy. We are sending transport coordinates."

The transmission ended abruptly. The viceroy's image faded, and the warbird's reappeared.

"Not very chatty," Riker commented dryly.

"Away team," Picard said. "Transporter room four." He lead Riker, Deanna, Worf, and Data to the turbolift, both relieved and energized now that the waiting was finally over.

Chapter 4

Picard watched as the *Enterprise* transporter room shimmered, then dissolved into what he assumed was the *Scimitar*'s observation deck. Lit only by the stars beyond, the chamber was dark— but as Picard's eyes began to adjust, he made out more of the away team's surroundings. The room was vast, empty of furniture save for a simple mat on the floor; the architecture was all upswept, lean lines with high ceilings: rather suitable for its tall, gaunt inhabitants. At one end, a bronze staircase led upward to a circular plate of transparent aluminum adorned with a design that reminded the captain somewhat of a mariner's compass.

A voice emerged from the shadows; a voice that Picard found disturbingly familiar, yet could not place.

"I hope you'll forgive the darkness. We're not comfortable in the light."

"Praetor Shinzon?" Picard asked.

The speaker moved toward them slightly, at which point Picard realized the chamber actually had been illuminated—

very dimly—for the low light glinted off Shinzon's uniform—a dark tunic that flashed the same deep purple color as his viceroy's.

Picard did not show his surprise, but beside him, Will Riker shifted slightly, and Worf let go a low hiss.

The praetor of the Romulan and Reman Empires was a human.

Even in the darkness, Picard sensed Shinzon staring intently at him. "Captain Picard," Shinzon said, in the same oddly familiar voice. "Jean-Luc Picard . . . I don't mean to stare, it's just—well, you can't imagine how long I've been waiting for this moment. . . I always imagined you taller, isn't that odd?" To Data, who was surreptiosly trying to study the readout from his tricorder, Shinzon said, "You may scan me without subterfuge, Commander Data."

As Data scanned, both he and Picard noticed the tall wraith-like figure of the Reman who had appeared on the *Enterprise* viewscreen; Picard got the impression that if the android made any sudden moves toward Shinzon, the Reman would attack like a guard dog.

"And you're not as we imagined you," Picard said frankly to Shinzon. There had been something strangely eager, almost fawning, about Shinzon's greeting.

"No?" Shinzon asked.

"You are human," Worf said gruffly.

"Commander Worf," Shinzon said graciously, then followed up with a Klingon phrase. Picard understood the gist to be that Worf was a brave warrior and a brother.

Worf replied tersely, in a tone of deep disapproval; he would save his greetings for a better brother.

Shinzon laughed, not in the least insulted.

Picard got to the point. "Why have you asked for our presence here?"

Shinzon did not answer; he had just fastened his gaze on Deanna Troi and seemed in a trance.

"Praetor?" Picard persisted.

Shinzon was too mesmerized by the sight of Troi to respond; he spoke only to her, his tone no longer commanding, but soft. "I've never met a human woman." He advanced slowly toward her, like one reluctant to startle a rare, precious bird.

"I'm only half human." Troi's manner was matter-of-fact; she appeared nonplussed by Shinzon's attentions.

"Deanna Troi of Betazed," Shinzon recited. "Empathic and telepathic abilities, ship's counselor. All of this I knew . . ." His voice dropped to a near whisper. "But I didn't know you were so beautiful."

Riker took a protective step forward. "You seem very familiar with our personnel."

Distracted, Shinzon ignored him and moved even closer to Deanna, his focus locked on her. "I am, Commander Riker." With the shy eagerness of a schoolboy, he asked Deanna, "May I touch your hair?"

Picard intervened. "Praetor," he demanded, "we've come to Romulus on a matter we were assured was of great importance. If you have anything to say to us as representatives of the Federation, I suggest you do so now."

But Shinzon's magnetic attraction to Troi seemed involuntary; he continued to stare at her with disquieting intensity. Troi handled it graciously, but Picard noted that she turned quickly toward the Reman called viceroy—who was watching the exchange with great interest—as if she sensed something strange occurring between Shinzon, the Reman, and herself.

"On the world I come from," Shinzon was telling Troi gently, "there's no light. No sun. Beauty isn't important. I see now there's a world elsewhere."

At the risk of an interstellar incident, Picard raised his voice. "Praetor Shinzon—"

With great difficulty, Shinzon withdrew his attention from Troi and at last turned back to Picard. Rather than bristle at the captain's sharpness, he smiled apologetically. "Yes, I'm sorry, Captain . . . There's so much we have to talk about."

"I would be interested to know," Picard remarked, his diplomacy tinged with dryness, "*what* we are talking about."

Light glinted off Shinzon's bald scalp as he moved and gestured with infinite enthusiasm, infinite passion. "Unity, Captain! Tearing down the walls between us to recognize we are one . . . people. Federation and Romulan. Human and Vulcan and Klingon and Reman. I'm speaking of the thing that makes us the same . . . We want peace."

Picard was too stunned to respond.

Shinzon continued, gesturing in the shadows. "I want to end the centuries of mistrust. I want to be your ally, not your enemy. As a first step, I propose we eliminate the Neutral Zone and begin a free and open exchange of goods and ideas."

Picard stifled his growing sense of hope and reminded himself of the *Scimitar,* lying cloaked for seventeen hours with her vast array of weaponry. Cautiously, he asked, "And the Senate supports you?"

Shinzon's tone was sere and hard as the desert wind. "I have dissolved the Senate."

A moment of silence passed as Picard and the away team absorbed this; then Shinzon spoke again, as if sensing the resistance to his words.

"Right now you're thinking this all sounds too good to be true . . . And you're wondering why the *Scimitar* is so well-armed. Is this the ship of a peacemaker? Or a predator?"

Picard glanced at him sharply. Was Shinzon a telepath? Or had he been spying on the *Enterprise* bridge and heard the captain's words?

Shinzon continued, shadows draping his features. "But you're also thinking the chance for peace is too promising to ignore. Above all, you're trying to decide if you can trust me. Am I right?"

"Yes," Picard said. He glanced sidewise at Troi; despite the dimness, he could tell she seemed just as surprised as he that Shinzon had so accurately gauged the captain's thoughts. So, Shinzon was not a telepath—but an uncanny judge of human character, despite his years separated from his own race.

"Then perhaps the time has come to add some illumination to our discussion," Shinzon said, with punlike emphasis on the word *illumination*. "Computer, raise lighting four levels."

Shadows vanished as the lights rose; for the first time, the captain could see the new praetor clearly.

And of the away team, Picard alone gasped aloud, to the confusion of the others. For he himself realized that he was looking at the very image of himself, Jean-Luc Picard, at the age of twenty-five.

But Shinzon understood. And with triumph in his eyes, he said, "Allow me to tell you a story that I hope will clarify my position . . . When I was very young I was stricken with an odd disease. I developed a hypersensitivity to sound. The slightest whisper caused me agony . . . No one knew what to do. Finally, I was taken to a doctor who had some experience with Terran illnesses and I was finally diagnosed with Shalaft's syndrome. Do you know of it, Captain?"

"You know I do," Picard said. The revelation of the new praetor's identity troubled him; far from being tempted to trust Shinzon more deeply, Picard instead felt wary, even hostile. He could sense the confusion of his officers at his reaction, but he kept his attention focused on Shinzon.

"Then you know it's a very rare syndrome. Genetic. All the male members of my family had it. Eventually I was treated. Now I can hear as well as you can, Captain." He moved toward Picard, who held his ground. "I can see as well as you can . . . I can feel everything you feel . . ." He stopped less than an arm's length until the two stood face-to-face. "In fact, I feel exactly what you feel. Don't I, Jean-Luc?"

Picard stared at the human praetor's features; it was like staring into a mirror, one that reflected a distant past . . . a past that had been stolen from him. For despite Picard's deep curiosity about his double, he felt a sense of violation as well. Here was the face he'd once had—here the gestures, the stance, the intonation. And—he had to admit it to himself—the arrogance.

"Come to dinner on Romulus tomorrow," Shinzon urged amiably. "Just the two of us . . . Or should I say . . . just the one of us."

Picard glanced at his crew: Riker, Troi, and Worf were all utterly confused by Shinzon's familiarity and their captain's barely repressed anger; and at Shinzon's next act, their confusion turned to shock.

The praetor calmly pulled out a deadly looking Reman knife and cut his arm, making sure the blade was coated with his blood. He then handed the weapon to Data.

"I think you'll be wanting this," Shinzon said cheerfully. "Tomorrow then, Captain. We have so much to discuss."

Picard narrowed his eyes and held his double's gaze as he pressed his communicator pin. "Picard to *Enterprise*. Five to beam up."

In the *Enterprise* sickbay, Picard stood next to Beverly as she pointed to the protonmicroscope reading from the Reman knife. Several other medical readouts were displayed, and Picard knew before Crusher spoke what they would reveal.

Riker and Troi flanked the two.

Beverly brushed back a stray wisp of hair as she straightened. "There's no doubt, Captain. Right down to your regressive strain of Shalaft's syndrome . . . He's a clone."

Picard tensed internally at the news. He thought he had already been prepared for it, but hearing it renewed him with fury, for reasons he had not entirely sorted out. "When was he . . . created?"

"About twenty-five years ago," Beverly answered. "They probably used a hair follicle or skin cell."

"Why?" Riker voiced the question that was already on Picard's lips.

"Believe me, Number One," the captain said heavily, "I'm going to find out. Contact Starfleet Command and inform them of the situation. I need to know where the hell he came from . . . Deanna."

He strode from sickbay, not looking behind him to see if Troi followed.

He did not have to. She was at his side immediately, reporting. "I would say he's been trained to resist telepathy. What I could sense of his emotions were erratic, very hard to follow."

"Is he sincere about wanting peace?" Picard asked. Odd, that he should have to ask that of one cloned from his own tissues, but he honestly did not trust Shinzon.

"I don't know." Deanna paused. "The strongest sense I had was that he's very curious about you. He wants to *know* you."

"Does he now," Picard said bitterly.

Troi put up a hand to stop him in midstride. "Captain, your feelings are appropriate. The anger I sense in you is—"

Her words opened a floodgate. "Can you imagine what it was like to stand there and look at him?!" Picard demanded. "To know an essential part of you had been *stolen?* I felt powerless . . . violated."

"What you're feeling is a loss of self," Deanna affirmed. "We cherish our uniqueness, believing that there can only be one of us in the universe."

"And now there are two." Picard seethed at the thought.

Troi laid a gentle hand on his wrist. "No, Captain. Biology alone doesn't make us who we are."

Picard looked up at her, considering this.

Aboard the *Enterprise,* it was night, but in Riker and Troi's cabin, Will was still hard at work, studying one of a series of padds scattered before him on the desk.

Deanna looked on him with tender concern. He had been like this for hours, devouring every scrap of information on Reman culture, Reman defenses—while muttering in frustration about the utter void of data on the new praetor, Shinzon.

Deanna understood Will's compulsion. She knew that at least part of his drivenness was due to his personality and professionalism; but she had also sensed the surge of jealousy that had overtaken him at Shinzon's blatant advances. And more than jealousy: Will was honestly worried that the praetor's interest in Deanna presented a danger. Subconsciously, Will was distracting himself from the jealousy and worry, keeping himself away from the ship's counselor until he was certain he had his emotions under control, lest they cause Deanna any concern.

She was touched by his desire not to trouble her. *Poor man*, she thought, *cursed with a Betazoid wife*. It would be near-impossible for him ever to hide anything from her. Yet she had promised herself that she would do her best *not* to intrude on Will's inner emotional life, unless requested to do so.

But some emotions—like the ones her new husband felt now—were too strong for her to blot out.

As for Shinzon, Troi was not particularly alarmed for her safety. True, he had been attracted to her to an extreme, disquieting degree, yet she understood: He was a young man, raised by Remans who were separated from their own females. The only women he had ever seen were Romulans, whom he despised.

Now, for the first time, he had seen a human (or at least, half-human) female. Young and in his prime, Shinzon reacted in expected fashion—by overreacting. It would have made no difference whether Troi or Beverly Crusher or any other human female officer had beamed aboard the *Scimitar*.

At the same time, there *had* been one small incident that planted a nebulous discomfort in Troi's mind. There had been a moment, when Shinzon had moved toward her, that she imagined she felt an attempt at telepathic communication— not by Shinzon, but by his Reman viceroy. Yet the sensation had been so subtle—and so fleeting—that she later decided it hadn't happened at all, that it had been the product of her imagination during an extremely intense moment. And so she had reported it to no one—certainly not to Will, who was still frowning at the same padd.

"Will," she said gently, "you need to rest . . ."

He squinted harder at the readout on the padd, the furrow between his dark eyebrows deepening. His focus was so intense he hadn't registered her presence or words at all, only that there was a distraction he needed to guard against.

Deanna raised her voice to a level not easily ignored. "As ship's counselor, I'm recommending you get some sleep."

Will heard her this time. He tossed the padd onto the desk, then drew a palm over his eyes and sighed as he looked up at her. "Some honeymoon," he said glumly.

Despite her own disappointment, she smiled and went over to him, then leaned down to kiss the side of his cheek, where the skin was clean-shaven. "Come to bed." She pulled him up from the chair; he rose easily, willingly, the crease between his eyebrows fading away.

"*Imzadi,*" he said, his lips curving upward in a soft smile.

They kissed. Deanna felt her own passion, and Will's, building. She pulled him backward across the deck until at last they fell back onto the bed.

In that instant, all thoughts of Romulans and Remans and the deadly arsenal aboard the *Scimitar* faded into the void. In Deanna's mind, she and Will were alone, adrift upon the Opal

Sea, their bodies supported by gently undulating waves. As her desire grew, she moved her arms, her hands, sensually around his body, caressing him, snaking her fingers through his hair. Her own hair, now straight and long, cascaded onto his cheek, and he lifted it to his lips and kissed it. She smiled; she knew he preferred her natural curl, but he was wise enough to do nothing but compliment her new style, knowing that she was bored. She pulled closer to him.

Her eyes were half open. In the space of a human heartbeat, no more, she watched as Will's hair between her fingers faded to nothingness, until she touched only scalp.

She recoiled at once.

There, on the bed, a smiling Shinzon lay in place of her husband. She put both hands upon his chest and tried to push away, but Shinzon held her fast.

"Imzadi," he whispered.

"No," she gasped.

He reached forward with a trembling hand—a stranger's hand—and stroked her cheek, the outside of his curled fingers brushing lightly against her skin. Deanna shuddered, repulsed.

"He can never know you as I know you," Shinzon breathed. "He can never touch you as I touch you . . ."

"This isn't real," Deanna countered flatly. Shinzon had found a way to force his way telepathically into her mind, but the body pressed to hers was Will's. She had to remember this, or surrender to horror . . .

"Can you feel my hands?" Shinzon asked, pulling her even more tightly to him. "Are they real? Can you feel my lips. . . ?" He pressed his mouth to her neck, causing her to rear her head back in revulsion.

Yet when he looked up at her again, his face was neither that of Shinzon's, or Will's, but of the fanged and ghostly viceroy's.

Deanna froze, yielding at last to terror as sharp claws grazed her skin in a monstrous parody of a caress.

From the Reman's corpse-pale lips came Shinzon's voice.

"I'm with you, *Imzadi*."

In a flash, the Reman metamorphosed into his praetor. Shinzon kissed her neck, her lips, her cheeks with wanton desperation. "I'll always be with you now."

"NO!" Troi shouted. With an act of infinite mental and physical strength, she pushed Shinzon from her mind and body.

"Deanna?!"

It was her husband's voice, her husband's body. Will looked tousled, bewildered, more worried than ever. For a long moment, Deanna stared at him, uncertain whether Shinzon or his viceroy would appear again; but the intruders were gone. Her mind was once again her own.

She threw her arms around Will and took comfort in the strong arms that enfolded her.

Inside the Romulan Senate Chamber, heavy drapes adorned the windows to prevent any hint of sunlight from entering.

At the moment, Donatra stood watching as her mentor, Commander Suran, was in conference with the new praetor and Senator Tal'Aura. Nearby, the Reman viceroy stood protectively eying Shinzon; Donatra watched the proceedings with no less attention. She still had the sense that there was something awry with the human. She knew the focus that was necessary in a successful praetor—and there was something distracting this one, something that he did not want the Romulan fleet to know. A weakness, perhaps; one that was now causing a delay which was close to causing disloyalty within the fleet.

Suran was permitting himself an open display of anger, pacing back and forth in front of Shinzon; it had been decided by the head commanders that a forceful message was necessary, in order to get the praetor to follow through with the promised plan. This act of supposedly making peace with a Federation envoy was pointless in the commanders' eyes, and could only serve some secret purpose of Shinzon's. Procrastination only allowed the Federation to prepare against attack.

". . . then I don't understand the reason for the delay!" Suran exclaimed.

Shinzon watched him with calm disdain. "You don't have to understand."

"And bringing the *Enterprise* here?" Suran paused in his pacing to turn his face toward the young human. "What possible purpose could that serve?!"

"I have a purpose."

Suran wheeled about so that he faced the praetor directly. "Then perhaps you will enlighten us—!"

Shinzon's pale face flushed a slight red. "Silence, *Romulan!*" His voice carried a depth of heat and hatred that startled even the confident Suran, and confirmed Donatra's suspicions: that the new praetor hated the Romulans desperately, and had no intention of dealing straightforwardly with them.

A tense pause followed; Shinzon glanced away and gathered himself, then said, more calmly, "You must learn *patience*, Commander . . . Do you know where I learned it? In the dilithium mines of Remus. Spend eighteen hours every day under the lash of a Romulan guard and you'll soon understand patience."

Carefully, Suran bowed his head and said in a subdued tone: "Praetor."

"Now go," Shinzon ordered. "I have some personal business."

Donatra began to follow the others, but Shinzon called after her.

"Commander Donatra, please remain."

She did as requested, turning to face him. Shinzon's stare was penetrating. Despite his humanness, he was attractive, with pleasing features if one ignored the brow and ears; oddly enough, he seemed to be sizing up her beauty.

Once the others had gone, he spoke, his tone more casual. "We talked about the power of words once, do you remember?"

"Yes, Praetor."

"Here's a word I would like you to consider . . . *allegiance*. It's something I demand from those who serve me."

So, Donatra realized, the praetor knew that he was in danger of losing the fleet by demanding such unquestioning loyalty in the face of his inexplicable delay.

"Do I serve you?" she asked simply.

"Yes," Shinzon replied, "and I think faithfully. Commander Suran, on the other hand, gives me pause."

Donatra hesitated. She sensed two things from Shinzon: first, a nobility, a deep sense of loyalty toward those he considered his brothers, the Remans. She could admire that: She, like Senator Tal'Aura and many others, had kept hidden their disapproval of the Empire's racist policies for many years. Shinzon had offered them hope that such policies would change.

Second, she sensed a bottomless hostility from Shinzon—a hatred, in fact, for her very own race, a hatred that the Empire had earned. Now that hatred threatened the fleet—and worse, her esteemed mentor, Commander Suran.

Donatra would do anything to protect her people; she would do anything to protect Suran. She would happily pretend to be Shinzon's spy; she would happily do more than that, to convince him that Romulans were capable of the finest emotions.

She lowered her voice, made it soothing, pleasing . . . "Here is another word, Praetor . . . *trust*. Do you trust me?" She circled him, moving ever closer. "How far does that trust extend? How deep does it go?"

She stopped in front of him, woman to man, so close she could sense the coolness of his human flesh. Shinzon stood immobile, breath quickening, but she could not read his eyes.

"What must a commander do to prove herself faithful to you?" she whispered, lifting a hand gently, touching the skin of his jaw. Its temperature was several degrees cooler than her own skin, and she imagined that to him, her fingertips radiated heat. "What must a woman do?"

Donatra drew in a silent breath of surprise at her sudden involuntary attraction to him. Here, in this human, was a sexuality long repressed, once coiled like a serpent and now striking forth, breaking free.

And like a serpent, Shinzon lashed out with considerable venom. He tore her hand from his face and spat, "You're not a woman, you're a *Romulan*."

Donatra fought and failed to keep the anger from her eyes.

He had despised her advances from the beginning; he had let her continue in order to humiliate her. Donatra took note: The new praetor was easily undone by his emotions, and arrogant enough to express his hatred to one who could otherwise be a considerable ally.

Perhaps arrogance and emotion, not strategy, were responsible for the praetor's current delay in carrying out the attack on Earth.

"*Now* we know each other, Commander," Shinzon said. "Serve me faithfully and you will be rewarded. And keep those lovely eyes on Commander Suran. At the first sign of treachery—"

"Dispose of him," Donatra offered, with the servility expected of her.

Shinzon gave an imperious nod. "Then you will have proven yourself. Now go."

Donatra bowed her head with feigned respect, then moved to leave.

"And Commander . . ."

She turned again to face him.

Shinzon's tone was matter-of-fact. "If you ever touch me again, I'll kill you."

She said nothing, only headed once more for the exit. In the doorway, she sensed movement behind her, and like any trained soldier, her instincts made her turn, wary of attack.

It was the ghostly viceroy, emerging from the shadows to attend to his praetor—but something odd about the exchange between the two men made Donatra linger to watch.

The viceroy put a gnarled palm firm against Shinzon's chest, then spoke to him in a low, earnest tone.

Donatra could not make out the words. The Reman language had been officially despised; no Romulan was legally allowed to learn it or speak it, and writing it, either phonetically or in the ancient script, was punishable by death.

Yet it became clear to her, in the split second before the doors closed, that the Reman was somehow ministering to the human, fulfilling some kind of need. Just what that need was, she could not fathom.

In Data's cabin, the B-4 sat quietly.

The one with its face had gone after instructing it to wait. This was consistent with its programming, and so it obeyed. Precisely *what* it awaited, it could not have said: but it knew neither patience nor impatience, and thus it simply sat.

Time passed.

Abruptly, circuitry sang. New programming arose, and compelled action. The waiting was over.

The B-4 stood and moved to a nearby computer console. It recognized the equipment and knew what it was to accomplish aboard the *Enterprise*. At a speed slightly faster than human eyes could follow, it began to punch in commands.

Chapter 5

That night, Picard found himself sitting at an elegantly appointed table in one of the last places he had ever expected to dine: the Romulan Senate Chamber. The cuisine had been surprisingly excellent; he had expected something spartan, as Remans had been forced to live off survival rations for so many centuries, but apparently the chef was Romulan, with interstellar sensibilities.

Shinzon had been too busy watching Picard to eat much. He sat across from the captain, his uniform gleaming in the dim light, his skin translucently pale: Certainly, Picard thought, he himself had been tan as a youth, his hair bleached lighter by Earth's sun, but there was still subtle differences in Shinzon's features—the very bones themselves—that could not be accounted for.

Only the area around the table had been illuminated so that the rest of the vast chamber was veiled in darkness; Picard could only wonder how many Reman guards lurked there.

But the overall effect was one of comfortable intimacy, and Shinzon was doing his best to maintain that atmosphere. Without the distraction of Troi, the young human seemly truly interested in Picard. Shinzon really seemed quite straight-foward and personable—even charming, Picard thought, then wondered whether his assessment was somehow conceited.

As angry as the captain had been upon his initial realization of the praetor's identity, he now experienced quite a different emotion: curiosity, even a desire to befriend. Yet he knew the latter emotion could be as harmful as anger to his mission, so he sought to strike a balance: congenial distrust.

Shinzon was talking: He seemed quite eager to share everything with his progenitor, to hold nothing back. ". . . and when I was ready they were going to replace you with me, put a Romulan agent at the heart of Starfleet. It was a bold plan."

"What happened?" Picard leaned forward, intrigued.

Shinzon shrugged. "As happens so frequently here on Romulus, a new government came to power. They decided to abandon the plan—they were afraid I'd be discovered and it would lead to war."

As Shinzon spoke, Picard poured himself a glass of Romulan ale from a delicate pitcher. He'd abstained during dinner, wary of a setup; but it seemed clear now that Shinzon's interest in him truly was personal.

Shinzon shuddered at the sight. "Romulan ale—I'm surprised. I can't stand it."

Picard smiled. "You'll acquire a taste for it."

The younger man did not reply. For a long moment, the two studied each other, without subterfuge, without defensiveness.

If I had had a son, Picard said to himself, then squelched the thought.

Shinzon's expression grew wistful. "It's not quite the face you remember."

"Not quite," Picard admitted.

A hardness crept into the Praetor's expression. "A lifetime of violence will do that. My nose was broken, and my jaw . . . But so much is the same. The eyes, you recognize the eyes."

"Yes."

"Our eyes reflect our lives, don't they? Yours are so confident," Shinzon said, and both of them reached for a carafe of water at the same instant.

Both stopped. Picard withdrew his hand.

"After you, Praetor."

Shinzon smiled dazzlingly. "Age before rank, Jean-Luc."

Picard grinned back and poured himself a glass. "So I'm not as tall as you expected?"

"I had always hoped I would hit two meters."

"With a full head of hair," the captain added. He knew this young man's hopes all too well.

Shinzon smiled again, amused. "There is that."

Picard paused, then pursued a grimmer subject. "How did you end up on Remus?"

"They sent me there to die," Shinzon said. Picard's question evoked painful memories; unbidden, the image of his first look at Remus—Black Hell—surfaced in his mind.

He had been seven years old: a child raised by unloving government scientists, Tran and Svana, but they had at least instilled in him a sense of purpose and pride. He would one day perform a great service for the Empire; he was destined to be a hero, to live with meaning, perhaps to die gloriously. He would be long remembered. Each season, his growth was marked by a message of greetings from the Praetor, whom he secretly thought of as father.

They called him Jean-Luc.

Then, quite suddenly, his world changed. One day the boy was studying in the room adjacent to the chamber where Tran and Svana worked. He heard the doors to the outer chamber open, heard Tran's deep voice demand an explanation. None came, only the whine of a disruptor followed by Svana's shrill scream. Another disruptor blast, an instant of silence, then heavy footsteps moving toward the boy's room.

The child called Jean-Luc did not run. He had been taught to abhor cowardice; besides, whatever Svana and Tran had done to displease the authorities could not possibly affect him, the Praetor's chosen.

He stood, small but unflinching, and eyed the armed centurions haughtily. When they seized his arms and dragged him away, he shouted, "The Praetor will see you killed!"

One centurion laughed aloud. "I think not. Your Praetor is dead, and the new one has no use for a scrawny human."

His sense of purpose thus stripped from him, the child was thrown upon a prison transport along with those who had committed minor infractions against the Empire, and were sentenced to guard the miners on the planet called Black Hell.

He had watched through the portal as the craft descended into darkness: The scene was straight from a nightmare. The only lighting came from torches shooting flame into the perennial night sky, revealing a desert valley encircled by mountains blacker than the horizon; nearby stood the vast mining operation, where ghoulish laborers hacked at rock with hand tools.

"How could a mere human survive the dilithium mines?" Shinzon asked himself; so vivid were the images that assaulted him that he had turned inward, half forgetting Picard. "I was only a child when they took me . . . I didn't see the sun and the stars again for nearly ten years . . ."

Down, down the depthless light shaft the human boy had ridden, and when it seemed they could go no deeper into the planet's core, the Romulan guard accompanying him opened the lift doors and brutally shoved the child out into the darkness.

The boy fell, terrified; around him, monsters—he had never before seen a Reman—tore glittering crystals from rock, while Romulans stood guard. To his young eyes, adult Romulans seemed amazingly tall; the Remans stood head and shoulders above them, pale sharp-fanged, sharp-clawed giants, with huge bony skulls.

Without warning, one of the Romulans aimed a weapon at one of the monsters, whose body, enveloped by the beam's glow, turned blindingly phosphorescent. The other monsters clutched their eyes while the victim writhed spasmodically in pain, involuntarily releasing a deep, soft groan.

The glow ceased; the victim dropped to his knees. But he recovered quickly, and went back to his labor with redoubled effort.

While the amused guards were distracted, something emerged from the shadows near the boy: the Reman named Vkruk. He looked down at the human a long moment, then took the boy's hand. In Vkruk's large, luminous eyes were compassion . . . and hope, and in that instant, the human raised by Romulans became the Reman liberator, Shinzon.

Together they moved down the mineshaft and into the darkness.

"The only thing the Romulan guards hated more than Remans was me," the adult Shinzon said. "But one man took pity on me: the man who became my viceroy. He taught me how to survive . . . And in that dark place, where there was nothing of myself, I found my Reman brothers. They showed me the only kindness I ever knew."

Shinzon returned from his reverie to the present, and stared past Picard at the Romulan crest on the wall. "For thousands of years the Romulan Senate has met in this chamber and dictated the fate of its sister-planet . . . But the time has come for us to live as equals."

Picard listened in fascination. Here was a man whose intellect had grown faster than his body . . . and whose emotions, like any twenty-year-old's, shone passionately on his face. Shinzon's deep hatred of the Romulans and equally deep loyalty toward the Remans was clearly unfeigned.

"You're doing this to liberate the Remans?" Picard suddenly understood.

"No race should be a slave to another," Shinzon said. "That was the single thought behind everything I've done: building the *Scimitar* at a secret base; assembling my army; finally coming to Romulus in force. I knew they wouldn't give us our freedom. We would have to take it."

"And how many Romulans died for your freedom?" Picard pressed, testing.

Shinzon's answer came a bit too abruptly, a bit too dismissively. "Too many. But the point is, the Empire is finally recognizing there's a better way. And that way is peace." Shinzon paused, searching his guest's face; he could not entirely mask the disappointment in his tone. "You don't trust me."

Picard thought of the *Scimitar,* of Shinzon's nearly uncontrolled response to Troi, of the murders that had most likely taken place in this very chamber. "I have no reason to."

"You have every reason," Shinzon said urgently. "If you had lived my life and experienced the suffering of my people . . . you'd be sitting where I am."

Picard refused to let himself be moved. "And if you had lived my life, you would understand my responsibility to the Federation. I can't let personal feelings unduly influence my decisions."

"All I have are personal feelings," Shinzon countered, then fell silent. Picard sensed there was something unspoken, a question that gnawed at his young doppelganger, one that was difficult for him to articulate. At last, Shinzon stated quietly, "I want to know . . . *what it is to be human.* You're the only link I have to that part of my life. The Remans gave me a future. You can tell me about my past."

"If I can," Picard replied, trying to repress a sudden surge of paternal feeling.

"Were we Picards always warriors?"

"I'm not a warrior, Shinzon. Is that what you think?"

The young man's confusion seemed genuine. "I don't know."

"I think of myself as an explorer."

"Then we were always explorers?" Shinzon asked eagerly.

"No." Picard's expression became rueful at the memory. "I was the first Picard to leave our solar system . . . It caused quite a stir in the family. But I had spent my youth—"

"Looking up at the stars," Shinzon finished.

Picard shot him a sharply curious look. "Yes."

Even in the dim light, the Praetor's eyes gleamed. "And you dreamed about what was up there. About—"

This time, Picard finished the sentence. "New worlds." For a time, the two stared at each other again. At last, Picard said candidly, "Shinzon . . . I'm trying to believe you."

"I know." The young man's voice was soft.

"If there's one ideal the Federation holds most dear," Picard said, "it's that all men, all races, can be united. From the first time the Vulcans came to Earth, we've sought a future of peace . . . Nothing would make me more proud than to take your hand in friendship. In time . . . When trust has been earned."

Shinzon's expression grew suddenly bland, unreadable. "In time, Jean-Luc."

After Picard's departure, Shinzon sat at the table, gazing at the ruins of dinner, when his viceroy entered.

"He's more gentle than I thought," Shinzon said, without looking up from Picard's unfinished glass of Romulan ale. "And he has a sense of humor." He had expected to glean information from his double; he had not expected to develop a sense of camaraderie and kinship. It would make what he had to do very difficult.

The viceroy grew stern, parental. "This was a mistake. We're wasting time."

"*My* time," Shinzon snapped. The viceroy had served as guardian and teacher when the human was younger—but the time for that had long passed. Vkruk needed to remember who was leader. "I'll spend it how I choose."

A tense silence ensued before the viceroy spoke again. "Don't forget our mission, Shinzon. We should act. Now."

The praetor released a deep, inaudible sigh and rose. He was human, and thus intrigued by the human who had given him life . . . *But*, he chided himself firmly, *my heart is Reman, and must remain so.*

"We'll return to the *Scimitar*," he said at last. "Prepare yourself for the bonding."

Picard stepped onto the turbolift to the *Enterprise* bridge with a sense of trepidation. Shinzon had been exactly what he had expected—and not. It would be easy to relax and let himself believe that the new praetor was emotionally the same as his progenitor; but Picard sensed something subtly different in Shinzon's emotional makeup, something as different as once-broken and slightly askew facial bones.

He's admitted that he's killed a number of Romulan Senators—a cold-blooded act I would never have been capable of. And the ship . . . the ship is more than just a deterrent. She's built to be used.

When the doors opened, Picard emerged from the lift to find Data, Worf, and Geordi waiting for him at the bridge engineering station—and judging from the looks on their faces, something was amiss on the ship.

As the captain approached, Worf said, "Sir, we've had an unauthorized access into the main computer."

Picard frowned. "Source?"

It was Geordi who replied. "It's going to take some time to find out—the data stream was rerouted through substations all over the ship."

"What programs were accessed?"

"That's what I don't get." Geordi folded his arms across his chest and shook his head. "It's mostly basic stellar cartography: star charts; communications protocols; some uplinks from colony tracking stations. It's not even restricted material."

Picard had no doubt this had to do with the new praetor; it increased his unease, even if the intrusion seemed innocuous enough. He turned to Worf. "Set up a security program to detect any unusual data stream rerouting. If it happens again, we want to be ready."

Geordi's tone was grim—so much so he gained Picard's immediate attention. "There's something else. I was reviewing the sensor logs." The engineer nodded at some readouts on his console. "When the *Scimitar* decloaked, there was a momentary spike in the tertiary EM band—there—" he pointed. "You're not going to believe this, but . . . it's thalaron."

Picard recoiled in shock. The *Scimitar* was more than just a predator, as he had said; indeed, she was a weapon capable of destroying the known universe.

In sickbay, Picard scowled at the readouts alongside Beverly Crusher, Data, and Geordi.

"I thought thalaron radiation was theoretical," Picard said, trying not to sound aghast.

Geordi gave a nod. "Which is why our initial scans didn't pick it up. But he's got it, captain."

"As I remember, thalaron research was banned in the Federation because of its *biogenic* properties." All feelings of friendship and optimism toward Shinzon had vanished; Picard once again felt a mounting sense of anger. Anger, oddly enough, at himself as well as Shinzon, as if he, Picard, were somehow responsible for the threat residing aboard the *Scimitar.*

Beside him, Beverly Crusher nodded. "It has the ability to consume organic material at the subatomic level . . . I can't overestimate the danger of thalaron radiation, Jean-Luc. A microscopic amount could kill every living thing on this ship in a matter of seconds."

"Understood," Picard said, though he in fact could not. How could a being created from himself risk developing such a deadly weapon? "Keep on it. I need to know what he has and how to neutralize any threat. Give me options."

He turned and left, sickened by the realization of what lurked behind the face that so looked like his own.

Seconds after the captain left, Data politely addressed Beverly Crusher. "Doctor, will you excuse us for a moment? Geordi, please come with me."

Crusher hardly paid any attention. She was too distracted by the medical displays, which graphed the effects the supposedly theoretical thalaron had on living cells: the dissolution rate was frighteningly swift, far more so than any other known radiation, and unlike other types, thalaron had no known prevention or cure. Its effects were penetrating and irreversible, making thalaron a scourge like the one nuclear radiation had been in the twenty-first century, before effective treatments were discovered.

Crusher thought immediately of her son, Wesley; only days ago, they had been laughing and talking together at Troi and Riker's wedding. The universe had seemed a safe and wonderful home then, a place filled with opportunity and joy: Wesley was settling into a real career in Starfleet, and she, Crusher, was excited over her new assignment in San Francisco.

Now the future seemed dark and unsafe, something no longer to be trusted. She did not, Crusher thought, like the idea of living in a universe that had thalaron radiation in it.

Later that night, Picard sat at his desk, scanning through an old album of holos. One of the images caught his attention and held it: a picture of himself as a serious-looking cadet on Earth's Starfleet Academy campus.

He had been so driven then, so determined to prove himself.

And he bore a chilling resemblance to the young man called Shinzon.

Could he, Picard asked himself, have been capable of the murders of the Romulan senators, of the development of such a hideous weapon as thalaron? If he had been taken from his own kind and brutalized, could he be capable of his double's deeds? Was he simply a product of a kinder, gentler culture?

The door comm chirped.

"Come . . ." Picard commanded absently, then glanced up at last from the image to see who entered, and immediately softened his tone. "Beverly, come in."

Beverly's smile was faint, the concern in her voice pronounced. "You're working late." She sat down beside the captain, her eyes focusing immediately on the image of Cadet Jean-Luc.

A part of the captain wanted to hide the picture, to change the subject, to state that he realized intellectually that he and Shinzon were two different entities, and that was that. But the wiser part of him knew he was deeply troubled by his clone's existence; the wiser part was grateful for old friends like Beverly, who knew him well and wanted to help.

So Picard let the image linger before them, and asked Beverly wryly, "Remember him?"

Her tone was light, dry; a corner of her mouth quirked upward. "He was a bit cocky, if I recall."

"He was a damn fool," Picard responded, with a sudden anger that surprised him. "Selfish and ambitious. Very much in need of seasoning."

Beverly's answer was firm. "He turned out all right."

Picard rose and went to the bulkhead window; beyond, the predatory *Scimitar* hovered. "I so wanted to believe Shinzon . . ." Hearing the wistfulness in his voice, he immediately hardened his tone. "But the thalaron radiation can't be explained away. Whatever he's after, it's not peace."

"Is he very much like you were?" Beverly asked gently.

Picard's reply was flat. "Yes."

Data's comm voice interrupted their conversation. "Data to Captain Picard—Geordi and I have identified the source of the unauthorized computer access. And, I believe, we have also discovered an opportunity to gain a tactical advantage."

"On my way," Picard said.

As he rose to leave, Beverly stood, momentarily blocking his path. "Jean-Luc," she said, "I've known you for over thirty years. I've watched you hold Wesley the day he was born. I watched you take your first command . . ." She glanced back down at the image of the young cadet. "Whoever you were then—Right now you're the man you made yourself. Shinzon is someone else."

Picard studied her a moment, then said with full candor, "Yes, Doctor, I want to believe that."

He exited, leaving her to gaze after him.

Early the following morning, Deanna Troi was alone on the turbolift, headed to the bridge.

It had taken her some time, after the incident with Shinzon, to reestablish a sense of mental security. The situation had proved even harder for Will, to know that his own caresses had taken on the feel of a stranger's—to know that his very touch had terrified his own wife. He had worked hard to deal with his hatred of Shinzon, lest it cause her more pain, but Deanna had insisted he express it. There was no point in trying to hide his emotions, after all; and at last he had admitted to her ruefully: *Here I call myself civilized. But all I want to do is kill him with my own hands.*

She'd tried to make a joke out of it: *I like my men a bit primitive.* But Will had been too upset to bring himself to smile.

So Deanna had prepared herself, in case of a second attack; she had been so used to opening herself mentally and emotionally to impressions that she researched and began to practice old Betazoid techniques for shutting herself off. It had comforted her—and, more important, it had comforted Will.

But that morning on the turbolift, she was entirely unprepared for the sound of Shinzon's voice calling her most private name.

"Imzadi."

A mere second before, there had been nothing in front of

her but empty air and the sleek turbolift doors. Now Shinzon stood before her, spreading his arms. There had been no sign of intership beaming—no sound, no materialization effect. This was another case of telepathic projection.

Deanna's voice was thick, shaking with anger. "You're not here." She said it as much to herself as to him.

"Very logical, Deanna," he said, as he moved to her; she pulled away—from his image, she reminded herself—but the turbolift left no room for escape. Shinzon continued. "But your heart doesn't constrain itself to mere logic . . ."

He slid a palm sensuously down the side of her neck, over the curve of her shoulder, then inside to her waist. He pulled her to him.

She fought back mentally, knowing physical effort was meaningless. Shinzon was not here. He was a telepathic projection of the viceroy. She was alone on the turbolift . . .

Yet the image, the feel, of Shinzon embracing her remained solid.

"Your heart longs to discover me. To know me . . ."

He kissed her. The warmth of his breath, the softness of his lips, his skin, brushing against her, seemed all too real. He drew back, his pale face flushed, his hazel eyes bright with desire. ". . . to leave this all behind and be with me."

Shinzon shoved her against the wall with a passion verging on brutality.

Deanna realized at once what he intended, and shouted, physically and mentally, "No . . ."

"I can feel your desire, Deanna . . ." Shinzon breathed.

She closed her eyes. With her entire mind, her entire will, she resisted.

The world around her began to dissolve, to bend, to transmute.

And she was aboard the *Scimitar,* where Shinzon knelt before a small flame. She herself knelt across from him—but she was far taller than he. He looked so human, so small, so frail . . .

She looked down at her hands: huge, white, with elongated fingers that tapered to sharp claws.

Shinzon looked up from the flame. "I can feel your hunger to know the Reman ways . . . the old ways . . ."

The world metamorphosed back to the turbolift; once again, Shinzon pressed against her, whispering: "Don't fear what you desire . . ."

But she had broken through the barrier once; she had seen her telepathic violator, and knew it to be the viceroy, not Shinzon. And so the arms she forced away, mentally and physically, were not the human's, but the long, ghostly ones of the Reman.

The image vanished. Abruptly, Deanna was alone on the turbolift.

Trembling, she sank to her knees.

Shinzon watched anxiously as the viceroy, entranced and kneeling before the flickering flame, suddenly stirred and lifted his head.

"The bond is broken," Vkruk said.

"Find her again," Shinzon commanded, fighting desperation. He was so close to consummating the relationship with Deanna . . . yet the entire day, he had begun to feel unwell.

It could not be beginning now, when he was so close to fulfilling his personal dreams.

To his frustration, the comm voice of one of his bridge officers interrupted them. "Praetor, we've received the transponder signal."

"On my way," Shinzon said firmly, seizing hold of his emotions. Deanna would have to wait. For now, there was important business to attend to if victory was to be achieved.

He rose—perhaps too quickly. Weakness and nausea overtook him; the room began slowly to spin. He swayed on his feet, struggling not to faint.

At once, he felt the steadying arms of the viceroy supporting him. Vkruk closed his eyes and laid a hand upon Shinzon's chest.

A moment passed; then the viceroy opened his eyes, his expression grim. "It's accelerating. You have no more time for games."

Shinzon sighed deeply. He honestly liked Jean-Luc Picard; in a perfect universe, where time was infinite, he might have persuaded Picard to become an ally.

"Have the doctors prepare," he told Vkruk flatly, then left.

Chapter 6

On the *Scimitar* bridge, Shinzon stood beside his two best engineers in front of a small transporter pad.

"Transport," Shinzon ordered, and one of the engineers obeyed.

As they watched, the B-4—a perfect replica of Picard's beloved Data—materialized on the platform.

"Welcome home," Shinzon greeted the android. He could not help congratulating himself for such a brilliant idea; not only had the B-4 served to lure Picard closer to the Neutral Zone, it now possessed all the data necessary to conquer Starfleet. Triumphant, Shinzon turned to his engineers. "Begin the download."

He watched, pleased, as they obediently opened the panel in the android's neck and began connecting computer conduits to the extra memory port there.

Content, Shinzon moved to a replicator unit. "Tea, hot."

A steaming cup appeared at once. Shinzon carefully sipped it as he watched his officers at work.

• • •

In the *Enterprise* sickbay, Will Riker watched with overwhelming concern as Dr. Crusher scanned Deanna with a handheld tricorder. Picard stood beside Will, who fought hard to keep his near-unbearable rage in check. It was not easy: he had been summoned to sickbay and arrived there to find Deanna fighting tears, more emotionally battered than he had ever seen her.

But, Riker knew, venting his fury now would serve no one but himself. It would make Deanna feel no better, and certainly wouldn't help the perilous situation they were in with Shinzon and his thalaron radiation.

Beverly finished her scan and told Deanna, "Aside from slightly elevated adrenaline and serotonin levels, you're completely normal." Her tone was soothing, but Riker took no comfort in it; it could not change the violence that had been wrought against his wife.

Nor did it seem to calm Deanna.

Picard asked gently, "Can you describe it, Deanna?"

She looked up at the captain; the unshed tears shining in her black eyes tore at Riker. Struggling, she said, "It was . . . a violation." She broke off, as if the words were simply too difficult to form. Riker took her hand; she gave him a grateful glance, then found the strength to continue.

"Shinzon's viceroy seems to have the ability to reach into my thoughts," she said. "I've become a liability . . . I request to be relieved of my duties."

"Permission denied," Picard said, with compassionate firmness. "If you can possibly endure any more of these . . . assaults . . . I need you at my side. Now more than ever—"

As he spoke, there came a faint mechanical hum; the molecules in the captain's body began to shimmer, sparkle, fade.

Riker slapped his combadge. "Worf! Raise shields!"

But it was too late. Picard had dematerialized, and Will Riker had no doubt as to where he had gone.

It would not surprise him later to learn that, in the instant after Picard disappeared, the *Scimitar* had cloaked herself, vanishing beneath the veil of space.

Picard found himself in what was apparently the *Scimitar*'s dimly lit brig; its main source of lighting appeared to be the shimmering force field that held him prisoner.

Beyond the field, Remans worked over a decidedly unpleasant-looking medical apparatus: a chair fitted with laser scalpels, intravenous tubing, and hyposprays. As Picard watched the preparations, Shinzon entered the chamber with the android in tow.

The praetor approached the brig at once, his attitude one of dangerous congeniality. Curiously, his once unmarred face was now covered by an intricate web of blue veins. "Hello, Jean-Luc."

Picard dispensed with civility. "Why am I here?"

"I was lonely," Shinzon began coyly, then at last noticed Picard's attention to the veins on his face. "Perhaps I'm not aging as well as you did." He nodded to a nearby guard, who at once deactivated the force field. Another Reman, apparently medical personnel, stepped into the brig and approached the captain with a hypospray.

Picard backed away. "What are you doing?"

"I need a sample of your blood," Shinzon said. "What do

your Borg friends say? Resistance is futile." Despite his attempt at humor, Picard heard the weariness, the coldness in his voice.

The Reman moved in swiftly; the claustrophobic brig afforded no place to hide. Picard let his blood be taken and cast a glance at the android behind Shinzon.

"Yes . . ." the praetor said, taking note of Picard's interest. "I learned there might be an existing prototype from a Cardassian historian, then went to a great deal of trouble to find it and scatter it about on Kolarus III. I knew it would pique your curiosity: a lure to make the *Enterprise* the closest ship to Romulus when I contacted Starfleet. The bait you couldn't refuse."

As he spoke, the Reman left the brig; the guard reactivated the force field. Picard watched as the doctor used the medical apparatus to analyze the blood.

"All of this so you could capture me?" Picard asked. Given Shinzon's sudden, peculiar aging, it made sense that he needed the captain for more than just conversation about family matters.

"Don't be so vain," his double countered scornfully. "After we found it, we made a few modifications. An extra memory port, a hidden transponder . . . I've now gained access to Starfleet's communication protocols. I now know the location of your entire fleet." Shinzon turned to the B-4. "You may go."

"Where?" the android asked, with childlike literalness.

Irritation crept into the praetor's tone. "Out of my sight." Shinzon watched the creature leave; lips twisting wryly, he told Picard, "It has more abilities than you might imagine . . . I've been training it to do little tricks for me like your robot does."

Picard had no patience for asides. "What's this all about?"

Shinzon spoke, and Picard heard the arrogance of the Cadet Jean-Luc—multiplied a thousand times, an arrogance that had been fed and never tempered by mistakes, by circumstance, by hard-earned humility. "It's about destiny, Picard. About a Reman outcast who—"

"You're not Reman," Picard corrected him swiftly.

Shinzon drew himself up as though he had been slapped. All efforts at charm vanished. For the first time, Picard saw the praetor's deep rage unmasked—a rage that crossed the barrier into madness. This man before him was not the young Jean-Luc, but a true stranger. "And I'm not quite human. So what am I? *My* life is meaningless as long as you're alive. What am I while you exist? A shadow? An *echo?*"

Picard spoke fiercely in an effort to pierce Shinzon's mania. "If your issues are with me *then deal with me*. This has nothing to do with my ship and nothing to do with the Federation."

"Oh, but it does," Shinzon retorted with heat. "We will no longer bow like slaves before anyone. Not the Romulans and not your mighty Federation. We're a race bred for war . . . for conquest."

Picard stared at the handsome young face on the other side of the shimmering force field, trying to understand how deeply hatred could change a life. "Are you ready to plunge the entire quadrant into war to satisfy your own personal demons?"

Shinzon's fury faded slightly, took on a glimmer of disbelief. "It amazes me how little you know yourself."

"I'm incapable of such an act," Picard stated flatly.

"*You are me*," Shinzon countered, with a fresh surge of anger. "The same noble Picard blood runs in our veins. Had you lived my life, you'd be doing *exactly* as I am . . . Look in the mirror, and see yourself." He stared piercingly at his prisoner. "Consider that, Captain . . . I can think of no greater torment for you."

As he turned to go, Picard spoke. "It's a mirror for you as well."

Shinzon wheeled about to face him, the pale skin beneath the blue spider veins flushed. Picard looked at him, past the rage, past the arrogance and posturing, at the young man who simply wanted to change the universe for the better.

For a heartbeat, no more, Shinzon stirred uncomfortably beneath Picard's probing gaze; for a heartbeat, no more, Picard sensed the young man waver and felt hope.

And then the shield of hatred and arrogance went back up; Shinzon's expression hardened, and he glanced over his shoulder, at the menacing medical preparations.

"Not for long," the Praetor said, then looked back at his double. With exaggerated deliberation, he turned his back to Picard and moved toward the door. "I'm afraid you won't survive to witness the victory of the echo . . . over the voice."

The *Enterprise* bridge was on Red Alert, with Worf at tactical and Geordi at the science station; a very tense Will Riker stood beside the latter.

"No response to our hails," the Klingon reported. Worf's muscles were coiled, ready for battle—a battle, Riker thought, they all knew was coming.

And all Shinzon had to do was expose them to a minute dose of thalaron radiation, and they and the *Enterprise* would melt into oblivion in less time than it took to draw a breath.

Some honeymoon, Riker repeated silently to himself; it had become his mantra of late, as the situation became more and more critical. Now he found no humor whatsoever in it—only a desperate wish that he could somehow wake from the nightmare and find himself adrift with Deanna on the Opal Sea.

But this was no dream. Riker watched as Geordi feverishly worked the science console. At last, the engineer turned to him in frustration.

"His cloak is perfect . . . no tachyon emissions, no residual antiprotons."

"Keep at it, Geordi," Riker said, with a calm he did not feel. "Find a way in."

He moved to the command chair.

"Sir," Worf called, with a frustration to match Geordi's, "we have to do something!"

Riker opened his mouth to call for a brainstorming session—but before he could utter the first word, Beverly Crusher, padd in hand, rushed from the turbolift and toward him with an urgency that caught his full attention. He had no doubt that it had to do with Picard and Shinzon.

"Will," she demanded, "I need to talk to you."

Inside the *Scimitar*'s brig, Picard stood frustrated, peering in vain at the edges of the glittering force field in hopes of finding a weakness. Not that it would do much good. The Reman guard just outside his cell was half again his height and armed, and the doctors swarming around the evil-looking surgical chair would certainly not fail to notice an escape attempt.

So Picard waited.

Only a few minutes passed before the android entered and

addressed the guard. "Praetor Shinzon wants the prisoner on the bridge."

The Reman pressed a control; the force field crackled faintly, then disappeared. As the guard released the captain and began to place restraints on his wrists, the android reached forward and swiftly incapacitated the Reman with a Vulcan neck pinch.

Picard breathed a sigh of relief.

"My mission was a success, sir," Data said. "I have discovered the source of the thalaron radiation. This entire ship is, essentially, a thalaron generator. The power relays lead to an activation matrix on the bridge."

"It's a weapon?" Picard asked, trying to grasp the dreadful enormity of the implication. A generator this size . . .

"It would appear so," Data answered simply.

"And the download?"

"He believes he has our communications protocols," Data said. "But they will give him inaccurate locations for all Starfleet vessels."

"Good work," Picard said.

Data rotated his left hand, then slid it forward, revealing a compartment in his wrist. From it, he carefully withdrew a small silver disk. Picard looked in appreciation at the Federation's newest, gleaming bit of technology—the ETU.

"Geordi supplied me with the prototype for the emergency transport unit," the android said. "I recommend you use it to return to the *Enterprise*."

Picard balked. "It'll only work for one of us."

"Yes, sir."

Picard shook his head. "We'll find a way off together." The

captain reinserted the ETU into Data's wrist, then handed the Reman guard's disruptor rifle to the android, while he hid the guard's smaller hand disruptor beneath his own tunic.

On the *Scimitar*'s bridge, Shinzon sat in his command chair. Normally, he would stand, as most of his soldiers did, eschewing comfort, but at this moment he was grateful for the rest. His body had finally turned on him, a gift of his former tormentors. The fatigue was crushing—but he would bear it, he promised himself grimly, just as he had borne his years in the dilithium mines. Compared to them, a short time of weakness was nothing.

At the same time that he battled weakness, he also fought a sense of shame. He should have been strong enough to stay down at the brig and watch Picard's death, an event that was no doubt happening now. He should be standing over his double now, gloating, watching as the captain's tanned face, drained of all its blood, grew as pale as his own.

No point in regretting it, Shinzon admonished himself. Picard's death was a necessary thing, and he did not permit himself to regret necessary things. After all, he hated the man—as a symbol of the crime committed against him, Shinzon, and against all other slaves of the Empire.

Even if the man was possessed of a certain nobility.

Thus, Shinzon sat on his bridge—where he was not needed for the moment—and waited for the summons from his Reman doctors that Picard was dead, and they were prepared to halt Shinzon's rapid degeneration.

The bridge doors opened; the viceroy emerged. "It's time for the procedure," he said.

Shinzon rose, and followed him off the bridge with something curiously like regret.

Wearing Reman hand restraints, Picard let himself be led out into the dark corridors of the vessel, prodded by his mock captor's disruptor rifle. The design of the interior, with its tall, lean lines and austere furnishings, reminded Picard more of a Zen monastery than a starship; but this was a temple dedicated to war.

Several Reman officers in uniform passed; all glared at the human prisoner with unmasked loathing. So: Shinzon's charm had masked an infinite hatred even Picard had failed to detect; and he had already instilled that hatred into his soldiers before even meeting his double. Millennia of prejudice against the "ugly," the frightening, Picard knew, had made his own species—including himself—judge the Remans' appearance as monstrous. Yet the bloodless face, the unusual height, the fangs, the claws—these were all traits bred into the race by the Romulans, who used their slaves as warriors. Picard studied the Remans and tried to understand; here was one eugenically engineered to kill, and viciously. Couple that with deep, eternal hatred born of enslavement and abuse . . .

He could understand, but he could never condone.

More Reman warriors appeared, glaring at Picard in disdain.

"Move, puny human animal." Data shoved the disruptor against Picard's spine—rather aggressively.

"A bit less florid, Commander," the captain advised, once the soldiers were out of earshot.

The words were scarcely uttered when they spotted Shinzon,

the viceroy, the Reman doctor and several technicians moving across an intersection. Immediately, Picard and Data flung themselves into a secluded corner as the group passed—thankfully, down the corridor and out of sight.

To the brig, Picard realized; their escape would soon be noted. Time was short. With increased alacrity, he and Data pressed on.

Accompanied by his entourage, Shinzon entered the brig with a sense both of exhilaration and of reluctance. There were many questions he still wished to ask Picard; yet at the same time, he was eager to regain his strength, to conquer this much-admired enemy, to move on with his plan of conquest.

But the force field in front of the brig was dark; and in its doorway lay the Reman guard, unconscious.

Shock and fury overtook Shinzon at once; he opened his mouth to shout an order, but for a long moment, no sound came.

Picard and Data were at that moment making their way swiftly through the *Scimitar*'s corridors; when the Klaxon began to howl, both broke into a full sprint. Over the sound of the alarm, commands were shouted in the guttural Reman tongue.

"This way, sir!" Data called, barely audible over the cacophony. "There is a shuttlebay ninety-four meters from our current location."

Picard followed him down a dark, twisting corridor—

And came to a full stop as a group of armed Remans appeared before them.

Without pause, Data fired the disruptor rifle, causing them to scatter; Picard quickly discarded his hand restraints and pulled the smaller disruptor from beneath his tunic.

The dark corridor blazed with light; beams burned through bulkheads, exploded circuitry in a shower of fireworks. Picard and Data ducked low, then ran down another corridor.

This one terminated in the shuttlebay door. First Picard then Data ran at the entrance—and promptly collided with the unyielding portal.

Data swiftly assessed a panel beside the door. "It seems to have an encrypted security system."

Rapid footfalls behind them; Picard turned to see a small army of Remans closing in on their prey.

Even worse: A second group of warriors approached from the opposite end of the corridor, sandwiching the two between Remans.

Without a hitch, Data tossed his rifle to the captain, who caught it with his free hand, pivoted, and fired—using both weapons, one aimed at each group.

As Picard fired and avoided blasts, Data used both hands to punch numbers into the security panel at inhuman speed.

"Alacrity would be appreciated, Commander," Picard shouted over the sound of explosions. Within one minute, perhaps less, one of them would no doubt be struck by a disruptor beam, permitting one of the groups to advance without restraint.

"They are trying to override the access codes," Data replied in a loud but aggravating calm voice. "Reman is really a most complex language with pictographs representing certain verb roots and—"

Picard, still weaving and shooting, cut him off. "While I find that fascinating, Data, we really need that door open!"

As if responding to his words, the doors slid apart.

As the two ducked down and backed into the shuttlebay, Picard kept up a barrage of disruptor fire. Once the door closed behind them, the captain fired a single blast, sealing the doors shut.

Picard turned. In front of them stood a fleet of streamlined, compact shuttles—*so* compact, in fact, that he wondered how a single Reman soldier could ever fit into one; it was less than half the size of the *Argo* land vehicle. But the vessels were made for two: a pilot, and a gunner to man the disruptor turret, with a transparent dome overhead that doubled as viewscreen and door.

They ran for the nearest vessel as Data called, "According to the ship's manifest, they are *Scorpion*-class attack fliers."

As Picard climbed in after Data, he could hear disruptor fire on the other side of the door: the Remans were trying to blast their way in.

The captain settled into the cramped cockpit of the tiny vessel; behind him, Data had already nestled into the gunner's station. The shuttlebay doors were beginning to char and black; in a moment, the Remans would be through.

Picard managed easily enough to power up the *Scorpion,* then stared down at the controls, marked in Reman and entirely unlike any Federation vessel he'd seen. He pointed at the nearest control. "What do you imagine this is?"

"Port thrusters, sir." Data hesitated ever so slightly. "Would you like me to drive?"

Remembering his comments about the captain's handling

of the *Argo*'s land vehicle, Picard shot him an evil look over his shoulder, then pressed the control.

The transparent dome closed a mere hand's breadth above the captain's head; the craft rose and hovered a meter above the deck. Its size made it extremely maneuverable; Picard swung it in an elegant arc to face the exit leading to space, and freedom.

"Can you open the shuttlebay doors?" he asked Data.

"Affirmative, sir . . ." The android quickly corrected himself. "Negative, sir. They have instigated security overrides and erected a force field around the external portals."

"Well then . . ." Picard's memory returned to the first time he had met Shinzon face-to-face. "Only one way to go."

He swung the tiny craft full about so she faced the internal doors, where sparks from the Reman disruptor fire were now visible.

Data turned to him. "Do you think this is a wise course of action?"

"We're about to find out . . . Power up disruptors and fire on my mark."

"Ready, Captain."

"Fire!"

An eye-dazzling burst emanated from the belly of the fighter and struck the inward doors, blasting them into infinitesimal, glowing bits of shrapnel. The *Scorpion* flew forward, into the corridor and past the stunned, scattered Remans.

There was not much time, Picard realized, before the *Scimitar*'s incredible technology would track them down and destroy them. Speed was essential; he could only hope that the *Scorpion* was as maneuverable as she seemed.

He drew a deep breath and went full throttle, past the startled Remans, banking sharply at the first hard curve. The vessel skimmed along the bulkhead with a screech of metal and rain of sparks, but Picard dared not slow. Round corner after corner he took the *Scorpion,* remembering a carnival ride he'd once taken on a holodeck as a child.

He made his way through the maze of corridors, hurtling at unthinkable speed, until at last, he found the chamber he sought.

With a nod, he directed Data; the disruptors blew the doors inward, and Picard piloted the vessel into the observation lounge, the place where Shinzon had seen his first human woman. The observation lounge — with its large circular window.

Another disruptor blast from Data, and the window exploded into shards that glowed red-gold from the beam's energy.

Picard maneuvered the *Scorpion* up the stairs and through the hole with room to spare; as he and Data flew into the infinite freedom of space, they shared a look of pure exultation.

Aboard the *Enterprise,* Will Riker kept reminding himself to relax and breathe; but after Crusher's explanation of Shinzon's desperate need for the captain, he and the crew had become—and remained—very tense and very silent. It was quite possible that by this time, the praetor had already murdered Picard—but, Riker encouraged himself, Data was also aboard that Reman vessel, and it was just as likely that the two of them were searching for a means of escape.

In the meantime, the bridge crew was still hard at work seeking a solution.

Riker was still mulling over Crusher's information when a glimmer on the main viewscreen caught his eye.

It was a craft. An enemy craft, a small fighter, no bigger than a gnat, and it seemed to appear out of nowhere.

Out of the *Scimitar*, Riker realized, and half rose as he shouted: "Worf! Lock on transporters!"

A half second later, Shinzon was on his feet. "Tractor beam! Now!"

But it was too late; the *Scorpion* flier shimmered into nothingness, and onto the *Enterprise*.

Shinzon gritted his teeth and fought not to howl.

"I have them, sir!" Worf shouted excitedly to Riker.

On the comm, Picard's order came through loud and clear.

"Number One, emergency warp!"

Riker was never so glad to obey.

And Shinzon, on his feet, all weakness temporarily forgotten, stared at his viewscreen. Against the velvet backdrop of space, the *Enterprise* powered forward and up, rolled over in a great arc—then disappeared in a blaze of light.

The brightness made the praetor and his soldiers raise a hand to their eyes.

Chapter 7

A short time later, Shinzon's troubles continued to increase. Mentally, he had forced himself to overcome the weakness, but the doctors had informed him that the degeneration rate was accelerating; soon it would overtake him with a vengeance, a fact made all too clear by the proliferation of blue veins across his face.

He forced himself to ignore it, and other signs of aging—as well as the sense of desperation at Picard's escape. But he could not ignore the image of Commander Suran now on his viewscreen.

Suran's white brows were drawn together in such a fierce scowl they almost met beneath his fringe of gray hair. The Romulan commander was furious, and daring enough to show it to his praetor. Or perhaps, Shinzon thought, Suran had forgotten himself and was merely addressing his praetor in the tone all Romulans reserved for Remans.

"This has gone far enough—!" Suran was actually shouting.

For the time, Shinzon maintained equanimity. "I thought we discussed patience, Commander."

"And mine is wearing thin!" Suran made the mistake of striking his console with his fist. It was a small, subtle sign of dominance, of implied violence, but it reminded Shinzon a bit too much of the Romulan guards in the mines. Once Suran's usefulness was over, the praetor decided, he would pay.

The Romulan continued in the same heated tone. "We supported you because you promised *action*. And yet you delay—"

Shinzon stood, and in unknowing imitation of his double, pulled down the edge of his tunic. "The *Enterprise* is immaterial," he countered forcefully. "They won't make it back to Federation space. And in two days the Federation will be crippled beyond repair. Does that satisfy you?"

The ripple of skin between Suran's eyebrows smoothed somewhat, and the crease there grew more shallow—but his expression remained distrustful. "For the moment."

Shinzon barely heard the reply; the whine of the phaser lash, the cracking of his own bones echoed loudly in his ears. He spoke with the unmitigated brutality he had experienced for most of his short life. "And when I return . . . You and I shall have a little talk about showing *proper respect!*"

Satisfied, he slammed his hand against the comm control, terminating the exchange.

But in the Romulan Senate Chamber, Donatra sat flanked by Suran and Senator Tal'Aura, and stared at the dark screen, anything but satisfied. She had been correct in sensing something missing from Shinzon: His obsession with his human origins had allowed Picard and the *Enterprise* to escape.

Worse, his attitude toward Suran showed that he was interested not in securing equality for all races, but in using his former captors, then turning the tables on them. No amount of reassurance would ever convince Shinzon that some Romulans truly disapproved of the Remans' enslavement.

Donatra broke the somber silence. "Does anyone in this room harbor any illusions about what he means by 'showing proper respect'?"

Suran remained silent, shaken.

Tal'Aura was still too aghast at what she'd seen on the viewscreen to answer the question. "What's happening to his face?" she demanded. Clearly, she was the consummate politician Donatra had judged her to be—interested only in using the new praetor as a swifter means to greater power. Now, for the first time, Tal'Aura was watching her dream age before her eyes. Shinzon had kept a medical condition from them: How much more was he hiding?

At any rate, Donatra still did not trust Tal'Aura enough to confide in her. But her mentor, Suran, deserved to hear the truth. She rose.

"Commander, a moment."

Suran understood her discomfort at speaking candidly in front of the senator. He followed her outside the chamber into the corridor.

Donatra spoke her mind at once; Suran—even though he was still the praetor's commander-in-chief—deserved no less.

"Are you truly prepared to have your hands drenched in

blood?" At long last, she let the passion of her hidden feelings show in her voice. "He'll show them no mercy. And his sins will mark us and our children for generations. Is that what it means to be a Romulan now?"

She knew Suran well. He did not respond, but listened intently: It meant he was still torn between two paths, not yet willing to commit himself to either. But at least he was hearing her words and weighing them.

Donatra pressed. "I think you should consider that question—or else you may have a lifetime to think about it in the dilithium mines."

She turned and left him to ponder all she had said. She was not afraid. There was a chance Suran would side with her; there was an equal chance he would side with the praetor. But in the latter event, she knew she could trust Suran to give her an honorable death, and a swift one.

Better yet, she knew her parents would have taken pride in their daughter's speech, and with that, Donatra was satisfied.

In the captain's ready room, where a breathtaking crystalline statue of the *Enterprise*-E now stood, Picard sat beside Riker and listened as Dr. Crusher briefed them both on the praetor's condition.

"The more I studied his DNA, the more confusing it got," Beverly said. There were shadows beneath her pale eyes, and Picard could hear the exhaustion in her tone. They were all tired, Picard included, but the situation was too grave to permit rest. "Finally I could only come to one conclusion: Shinzon was created with temporal RNA sequencing. He was designed so that at a certain point his aging process could be accelerated to reach your age more quickly, so he could replace you."

"But the Romulans abandoned the plan," Picard thought aloud.

Beverly continued the train. "As a result, the temporal sequencing was never activated. Remember, he was supposed to replace you at nearly your current age. He was *engineered* to skip thirty years of life. But since the RNA sequencing was never activated, his cellular structure has started to break down . . ." She paused to soften her tone. "He's dying."

"Dying?" To his surprise, Picard felt the one emotion the bloodthirsty praetor did not deserve: pity.

"He wasn't designed to live a complete, human life span," Riker added.

Picard glanced at his second-in-command, then back to the doctor. "Can anything be done for him?"

Beverly shook her head with honest regret. She, too, seemed to feel an unwarranted desire to help Shinzon. "Not without a complete myelodysplastic infusion from the only donor with compatible DNA . . . But that would mean draining all your blood."

Picard thought of the gruesome medical station in the *Scimitar*'s brig, and Shinzon's cavalier insistence that the captain die. But Picard had not realized, then, that Shinzon had truly had no choice if he were to survive. Quietly, the captain asked, "How long does he have?"

"I can't say," Beverly replied, eyeing him steadily, "but the rate of decay seems to be accelerating."

Picard considered this, then said with full certainty, "Then he'll come for me."

• • •

In his cabin, Data stood studying the B-4 with keen interest.

His double had been deactivated: For the first time, Data saw what he himself looked like in the same condition—lifeless, motionless. He suspected that, were he capable at the moment of emotion, he would find the sight disturbing. Perhaps it would be comparable to a human being seeing him- or herself in death.

He opened a panel in the B-4's neck and used a small device to activate his double's head.

At once, the B-4's amber eyes opened and became cognizant. It caught Data's gaze at once. "Brother . . . I cannot move."

"No," Data said. "I have only activated your cognitive and communication subroutines."

"Why?"

"Because you are dangerous."

"Why?"

"You have been programmed to gather information that can be used against this ship," Data explained.

"I do not understand," the B-4 said.

"I know." Data paused, then asked the required questions. "Do you know anything about Shinzon's plans against the Federation?"

"No."

Data did not doubt the android's veracity; it had not been programmed to deceive, merely to devour information and relay it. "Do you have any knowledge of the tactical abilities of his ship?"

"No," the B-4 answered. "Can I move now?"

"No." Data manipulated his instrument to adjust the circuitry in his double's neck.

"What are you doing?" the B-4 asked.

"I must deactivate you."

"For how long?"

"Indefinitely," Data replied.

"How long is that?"

Data paused in his work and gazed steadily into the eyes that mirrored his own. "A long time, brother."

He turned the instrument; the animation in the B-4's eyes faded to blankness.

For a time, Data stood before him and wondered whether death was the same for humans.

While the *Enterprise* was en route to its rendezvous with the best of Starfleet, Picard assembled all of his senior officers at the large conference table in the observation lounge. The lights were lowered, in deference to Earth's night—even so, after Picard's stay on the *Scimitar,* they seemed comfortingly bright. Yet they could not dispel the sense of heaviness that permeated the room. The *Enterprise* was going into battle—a battle she could not technologically win.

At the moment, Geordi La Forge was briefing the officers on the very phenomenon that would likely prove their doom.

"It's called a cascading biogenic pulse," Geordi said. "The unique properties of thalaron radiation allow the energy beam to expand almost without limits. Depending on the radiant intensity, it could encompass a ship . . . or a planet."

"He would only have built a weapon of that scope for one reason," Picard stated flatly. "He's going after Earth."

Deanna turned to him. She had, Picard noted, recovered from Shinzon's telepathic assault with a determination and resiliency that were remarkable. "How can you be certain?"

Picard's lips thinned slightly in something less than a smile. "I know how he thinks."

Will Riker nodded, grasping the implication. "Destroy humanity, and the Federation is crippled . . ."

"And the Romulans invade," Picard finished.

A grim beat of silence passed; then Riker asked Geordi, "There's no way to penetrate his cloak?"

La Forge's reply was adamant. "No, sir."

Riker scowled in frustration. "He could pass within ten meters of every ship in Starfleet and they'd never know."

"But we do have one advantage." Beverly turned to the captain. "He needs your blood to live. He might come after you first."

"I was counting on it," Picard said. "We've been ordered to head to sector one-oh-four-five. Starfleet is diverting the fleet to meet us there."

"Strength in numbers?" Will asked quizzically; they all knew that with thalaron radiation, more ships simply meant more victims.

"We can only hope so." Picard paused to somberly study each of his officers in turn. "He can't be allowed to use that weapon. All other concerns are secondary . . . Do you understand me?"

From the grim expressions around the table, it was clear each person did. The *Enterprise*—and all aboard her—were expendable.

Riker spoke for all of them. "Yes, sir."

Picard stood and pressed his comm button. "All hands . . . Battle stations."

• • •

Captain's Personal Log, Supplemental. We're heading toward Federation space at maximum warp. The crew has responded with the dedication I've come to expect of them . . . And like a thousand other commanders on a thousand other battlefields throughout history, I wait for the dawn.

It had been a long night aboard the *Enterprise,* and it was yet to be over. Picard had wandered his ship like a restless spirit, offering aid where it was needed, encouragement where there was anxiety. In one corridor, he had encountered a young ensign—fresh-faced, recently out of the Academy— her eyes bright with fear.

He had stopped and spoken to her, inquired after her assignment, complimented her on her handling of it. He had reminded her of the other officers working as hard as she was: Commanders Riker and Worf in charge of tactical; Commander Data, analyzing every shred of information on the praetor's ship; Engineer La Forge, adding an extra layer of force fields around the warp core. And all over the ship, security officers were distributing phasers.

We have the best ship, the best crew in Starfleet, Picard had told the ensign. *And we are prepared for anything.*

He did not finish his thought aloud: Anything, that is, except thalaron radiation.

No degree of preparation could make the *Enterprise,* or the entire fleet for that matter, invulnerable to it. Picard could only hope that the *Scimitar,* a spaceborne weapon, was meant to be deployed once—in the presence of Earth. But even without Shinzon's use of thalaron, the *Enterprise* was no match for the *Scimitar*.

Only one thing could save the *Enterprise,* the fleet: Shinzon's humanity. Picard had tried and failed to touch it, but he knew, instinctively, that there was *some* way to get through. Some way to touch the core of Shinzon's essence, to prevent the monstrous fate they now faced.

And so, Picard left the young ensign, the terror now faded from her eyes. He himself was less hopeful; he continued to haunt the ship's corridors, looking for a place to be useful, mulling over how to touch Shinzon's soul across the vastness of space.

The captain made his way to sickbay.

As the doors closed behind him, he stood and watched Dr. Crusher and her team hard at work, positioning antigravity gurneys, readying surgical supplies—preparing for the carnage to come. All this because of a few errant cells stolen from Picard years ago.

He quickly squelched the mental image of sickbay filled with the injured and dying, and looked on as a security officer handed Crusher a phaser.

She took it matter-of-factly, then glanced up and caught sight of the captain. She moved toward him at once, holstering the weapon smoothly, as if it were something she did every day.

The sight was troubling. " 'To seek out new life, and new civilizations . . .' " Picard recited quietly when she arrived at his side. "Zephram Cochrane's own words . . . When Charles

Darwin set out on the *H.M.S. Beagle,* on his journey into the unknown he sailed without a single musket."

Beverly's tone was gentle. "That was another time."

"How far we've come," Picard said bitterly, then released a silent sigh and spoke this time with genuine concern. "Let me known if you need anything."

She gave a slight nod; he moved to exit. Beverly called after him.

"Jean-Luc . . ."

He turned, expectant.

She spoke with remarkable conviction, each word emphatic. "He is not you."

He paused, held her gaze a long moment, then left.

Shinzon sat in his command chair on the *Scimitar,* struggling not to gasp; he was grateful he could not see the signs of aging on his own face.

He took a seven-year-old child's comfort in the presence of his viceroy, who once again stood with his palm pressed firmly to Shinzon's chest, his head low.

"How long?" Shinzon demanded.

Vkruk never lied to him, of softened the blow. "A matter of hours now—" The Reman lingered near his master, as if yearning to offer more comfort.

Shinzon shoved him away and stood, but the viceroy hovered nearby.

"You must begin the procedure now," the Reman insisted.

Shinzon slammed a fist against the arm of his chair, furious with it all: with Picard for escaping, with Vkruk, for telling him what he already knew, with his own body, for betraying him—and most of all, with the Romulans, for designing him to react in this manner. He would survive, Shinzon promised himself grimly—he *had* to survive, for he had a new plan . . .

And he would not permit his body or Vkruk's concern force him to move too soon.

Shinzon struggled with his anger, mastered it, and gathered himself. Calmly, he sat back down and in an even tone asked his second-in-command, "How long until we reach the rift?"

The viceroy moved to the nearest console and glanced at it briefly. "Seven minutes."

Shinzon settled back in his chair, pleased. He could easily endure another seven minutes. Satisfied, he gazed at the promising tableau on his viewscreen: the *Enterprise,* so close he felt he could stretch forth his arm and touch her; in the distance beyond lay the Bassen Rift, a breathtaking moving gem of energy bursts, snaking like opalescent lightning through fog. Shinzon squinted, hopeful, at the crackling play of turquoise, pale rose, white.

Meantime, Picard had made his way to engineering, where Data worked at a monitor displaying cartographic projections of star systems. In the background, the warp core hummed quietly, a sound that the captain had always found soothing.

"Show me our current position," Picard commanded.

Data complied; the monitor image shifted to the current sector, with a blip indicating the *Enterprise*.

Picard took note. "How long until we reach the fleet?"

"At our current velocity, we will arrive at sector one-oh-four-five in approximately forty minutes." Data pressed another control. The image changed again to reveal the aforementioned sector, where several blips indicated Starfleet vessels moving into position.

Picard gazed at the sight for a moment, then quoted softly, " 'For now we see but through a glass darkly . . .' "

Data shot him a quizzical glance. "Sir?"

"He said he's a mirror."

"Of you?"

"Yes."

Data tilted his head, considering it. "I do not agree. Although you share the same genetic structure, the events of your life have created a unique individual."

"And if I had lived his life?" Picard persisted. "Is it possible I would have rejected my humanity?"

"No, sir, it is not possible," Data said. "The B-four is physically identical to me, although his neural pathways are not as advanced. But even if they were, he would not be me."

Picard wanted to believe. "How can you be sure?"

"I aspire, sir," the android answered confidently. "To be better than I am. The B-four does not. Nor does Shinzon."

For the first time since learning the practor's real intent, the weight of Picard's guilt lifted; ironic, that Data, a mass of circuitry and programming, could so eloquently express the difference between one human spirit and another. He paused. "We'll never know what Shinzon might have been. Had he stood where I did as a child . . . and looked up at the stars."

The captain's words lingered in the air for a moment; then the image on Data's monitor sputtered with static. The android pressed several controls.

"We are passing through the Bassen Rift," he said. "The projection will return when we have cleared it."

"It's interfering with our uplink from Starfleet cartography?" A sense of ominousness overtook Picard; he suddenly understood what Shinzon had been waiting for.

"The rift affects all long-range communications—" Data began, but Picard had already pressed his combadge.

"Commander Riker, evasive maneuvers!"

Too late. The deck beneath Picard's feet shuddered, then with a thunderous roar pitched hard to one side; he went tumbling headfirst into consoles and equipment, colliding with Data's limbs and torso. With his peripheral vision, he watched as the warp core flickered erratically, and knew that Shinzon was trying to disable the ship.

Picard grabbed the edge of the console, righting himself— only to be thrown to one side again by a second strike, a third; the warp core brightened dramatically, then dulled. With a furious lurch, the *Enterprise* dropped out of warp.

Shinzon watched the disruptor fire with satisfaction. "Target weapons systems and shields," he told his weapons officer. "I don't want the *Enterprise* destroyed."

On the viewscreen, dazzling blasts seared from beneath the *Scimitar* and made their way precisely to the target on the Federation ship. Shinzon smiled faintly, and spoke to someone who could not hear him, but nonetheless knew exactly what he was saying.

"Can you learn to see in the dark, Captain?"

With Data following, Picard emerged on unsteady legs from the turbolift as the *Enterprise* took another blow. He went directly to Riker, who rose from the command chair.

"Report."

"He's firing through his cloak," Will said. "We can't get a lock."

From the engineering station, Geordi called over the rumbling blast. "He disabled our warp drive with his first shot. We've only got impulse."

"Long-range communication is impossible as long as we're in the Rift—" Worf began, then fell silent, holding onto his console as the deck pitched again to the sound of thunder.

"Worf," Picard ordered, "prepare a full phaser spread, zero elevation. All banks on my mark. Scan for shield impacts and stand by photon torpedoes."

"Aye, sir," Worf called.

Another blast; the ship reeled again.

"Fire," the captain shouted.

The *Enterprise*'s entire bank of phasers streaked into space; for an instant, the *Scimitar*'s shape was illuminated as one of her shields took a hit.

Immediately after, photon torpedoes followed . . . but passed harmlessly through a void where the *Scimitar* had once been.

Shinzon was gloating. "You're too slow, old man . . ." He began punching commands directly into the control panel of his chair console. "Attack pattern Shinzon Theta."

He watched, a small, malevolent smile on his lips as the invisible *Scimitar* ran straight over the *Enterprise,* firing down on her at close range.

• • •

The bridge shook violently under the attack; Picard could scarcely remain in his chair, could scarcely hear Data reporting in full voice:

"We are losing dorsal shields—"

"Full axis rotation to port! Fire all ventral phasers!" Picard commanded.

The *Enterprise* rolled onto her back, firing up at the invisible ship that the captain knew had to be there. Only a few shots struck, illuminating the *Scimitar*'s underside fleetingly.

"Minimal damage to the *Scimitar,* " Worf reported.

"Defensive pattern Kirk Epsilon," Riker told the helm. "Geordi, get those shields online."

It had not been enough, Picard knew; nothing the *Enterprise* could do would be enough. The *Scimitar* had her totally outgunned, outmaneuvered. She and her crew had no chance of surviving—unless, Picard's instincts nagged at him for the hundredth time, he could find a way to touch Shinzon's humanity. But how—?

Inspiration struck Picard in a way he had not foreseen. He would touch Shinzon indeed, but not with appeals for compassion. He touched his combadge. "Counselor Troi, report to the bridge."

Riker turned to him, frustrated. "Unless we can disable his cloak, we're just going to be firing in the dark."

"Agreed," Picard said—but he had just decided that there was more than one way to get past a cloaking device.

"Sir," Worf reported, "we're being hailed."

"On screen."

Shinzon appeared—as Picard had expected—looking even more haggard but exceptionally smug; he had already decided his enemy had been defeated. "Captain Picard," he said amiably, "will you join me in your ready room?"

In the ready room, Picard watched as the shimmering light, reflected in the crystal statue of the *Enterprise,* transformed into a deceptively solid-looking Shinzon—until that is, the praetor walked *through* Picard's desk. Shinzon stood straight and behaved with his usual confidence—but Picard sensed the weakness in every word, every gesture. The younger man was using every ounce of will and strength to hold himself up, to appear normal—but the premature aging had already taken a bizarre toll on his features. What was happening to him internally?

"You can't trace my holographic emitters, Captain. So don't bother . . . And you can't contact Starfleet. It's just the two of us now, Jean-Luc, as it should be . . ."

"Why are you here?" Picard demanded.

"To accept your surrender," Shinzon said with mock graciousness. "I can clearly destroy you at any time. Lower your shields and allow me to transport you to my ship."

"And the *Enterprise?*"

"I have little interest in your quaint vessel, Captain. If the *Enterprise* will withdraw to a distance of one hundred light years, it will not be harmed."

Picard hid neither his anger nor his disgust. "You know that's not possible."

"I know . . . You'll all gladly die to save your homeworld."

"Look at me, Shinzon!" Picard urged, his tone, his gaze intense. "Your eyes, your hands, your heart, the blood pumping inside you, are the same as mine. The raw material is the same! We have the same *potential*—"

The praetor waved a hand dismissively. "That's the past, Captain—"

"It can also be the future. Buried deep inside you—beneath the years of pain and anger—is something that has never been nurtured: the potential to make yourself into a better man . . . To make yourself more than you are. *That's* what it is to be human." Picard faced him relentlessly, refusing to surrender this part of himself to the dark. "Yes . . . I know you . . . There was a time you looked at the stars . . . and dreamed of what might be."

Shinzon dropped his gaze, turned one sculpted cheekbone away; all arrogance ebbed from his tone. "Long ago."

"Not so long," Picard said.

A glimmer of frustration, of repressed fury, passed over the young man's features. He hardened his demeanor. "Childish dreams, Captain . . . Lost in the dilithium mines of Remus. I'm what you see now."

"I see more than that . . ." Picard took a step toward the image. "I see what you could be."

Projection or not, Shinzon instinctively backed away from his double as Picard continued to move closer.

"The man who is Jean-Luc Picard *and* Shinzon of Remus won't exterminate the population of an entire planet!" the captain insisted. *"He is better than that!"*

"He is what his life has made him!" Shinzon cried, clearly in turmoil.

Picard felt a fresh surge of hope. Quietly, he asked, "And what will he do with that life?"

Shinzon stared at him in confusion.

"If I were to beam to your ship . . ." Picard continued,

"let you complete your medical procedure, give you a full life . . . What would you do with the time?"

Again, the young man dropped his gaze; he did not reply.

"If I gave you my life, what would you do with it? Would you spend the years in a blaze of hatred as you do now?"

"I don't know," Shinzon said. Picard believed him; all cockiness, all confidence was gone.

"You once asked me about your past," the captain said. "Your history. Let me tell you about mine . . . When I was your age, I burned with ambition. I was very proud and my pride often hurt people. I made every wrong choice a young man can . . ." He shook his head in rueful remembrance. "But one thing saved me . . . I had a father who believed in me. Who took the time to teach me a better way . . ." He shot Shinzon a pointed look. "You have the same father."

Shinzon was mesmerized; and there, Picard thought, hung the fate of billions of lives. He spoke quietly, tentatively. "Let me tell you about our father."

Shinzon looked up, his eyes filled with such aching sorrow that for an instant, Picard thought he might weep. "That's your life," he whispered. "Not mine . . ."

Picard reached forth a hand. "Please . . ."

"It's too late." Shinzon shuddered—whether from emotional pain or physical, the captain could not tell.

"Never! . . . Never . . . You can still make a choice!" Picard insisted. "Make the right one now!"

"I can't fight what I am!" Shinzon cried, his voice ragged.

"You can!"

Shinzon backed away, allowing the sadness to turn again to rage. "I'll show you my true nature. *Our* true nature. And as

Earth dies—remember that I'm forever Shinzon of Remus! And *my* voice will echo through time long after yours has faded to a dim memory."

His image shimmered, then faded.

Picard stood alone, with a sense of defeat. He had wanted to save Shinzon, to befriend him—now he was forced to take the one action he had wanted to avoid: to fight him as an enemy, to the death.

Chapter 8

Shinzon strode to his command chair, allowing his fury full rein.

It was his rage, after all, that had saved him from succumbing to the wounds inflicted on him in the mines; his rage that had taken him from slave of the Empire to its praetor. He was ashamed now that Picard had dug beneath that anger and found the hopeful young boy. There lay softness, weakness, compassion: the traits that would undo all that Shinzon had fought to accomplish, the traits that would now prove the undoing of Jean-Luc Picard.

Shinzon was furious at himself for other reasons: He should have taken Vkruk's advice and destroyed Picard the first instant the captain set foot aboard the *Scimitar*. Instead, Shinzon had yielded to a very human impulse: curiosity. Even more horrific, a part of him had wanted to befriend his double, to win approval—all this while knowing he had no choice but to kill Picard.

Shinzon's self-loathing increased as he realized the truth: He had delayed Picard's death, delayed the battle with Starfleet and the destruction of Earth—all because he had *liked* Jean-Luc, and had not wanted him to die. For a dizzying second, he had permitted the captain's words to move him emotionally. He had *almost* reconsidered—

Bitterly, Shinzon broke off the train of thought and took his chair, shouting at his viceroy, "Disable their weapons!"

The Reman began to move—then stopped, as another officer called out: "Two ships decloaking, sir—*Romulan!*"

Shinzon swung about in his chair and stared at the viewscreen, utterly startled by the sight. Two Romulan warbirds now flanked the *Enterprise*. But this simply could not be—he had given Suran clear instructions that all ships were to await his signal to attack. They had no business decloaking here, in the Bassen Rift . . .

Only seconds after Shinzon settled into his command chair, Picard took his own, noting that Deanna Troi had obeyed the order to report to the bridge. Two Romulan warbirds had moved into positions alongside the *Enterprise*.

"Just when I thought this couldn't get any worse," Riker said dryly at Picard's side. In the midst of mortal danger, Picard thought, only Will could maintain a sense of humor.

Picard clutched the arms of his chair, steeling himself for a triple barrage of disruptor fire that would swiftly disable his ship—but the deck remained blessedly stable beneath him.

Worf spoke, now audible using a normal tone of voice. "We're being hailed."

Picard sighed. No doubt this was a second round of threats

insisting he hand himself over—but he could not give Shinzon life to continue his mad plan. "On screen."

The image that appeared was that of a handsome, surprisingly young female. Her features were quintessentially Romulan: almond eyes beneath fiercely upward-slanting eyebrows, all framed beneath a sleek cap of jet-colored hair. There was a sharp intelligence, a straightforwardness to her that made Picard like her at once, enemy or no.

"Captain Picard," she said, with genuine politeness. "Commander Donatra of the *Warbird Valdore*. Might we be of assistance?"

"Assistance?" Picard was momentarily too stunned to do anything but repeat the word.

One corner of the commander's mouth quirked ruefully to the side; clearly, she felt apologetic toward the Federation captain, and rather disgusted that the present situation had been allowed to get so far out of hand. "The Empire considers this a matter of internal security. We regret you've become involved."

For half a heartbeat, Picard could only look at her in amazement; then, with as much honest warmth as he had ever felt toward any being, he told her: "When this is over, I owe you a drink."

The viewscreen flickered suddenly with static; over the comm link came the roar of disruptor fire. On screen, the *Valdore* bridge rocked. Donatra held fast to her chair, and when the attack had passed, she said, with merely the suggestion of a smile in her eyes, "Romulan ale, captain. Let's get to work. *Valdore* out."

Were she not a Romulan, and already in command of a vessel, Picard thought, he would gladly request her as his new second-in-command. With renewed hope, he turned to Worf. "You heard the lady. Get to work."

The *Enterprise* powered forward into battle.

Picard watched the viewscreen as a blinding barrage of white phaser and disruptor fire from the three allied ships illuminated the *Scimitar* in brief bursts. Its outline flickered in and out of view, a dazzling ghost.

Picard turned to Worf. "Coordinate our attack with the *Valdore*'s tactical officer. Triangulate fire on any shield impacts."

"Aye, sir."

The captain grasped the arms of his chair as the ship rocked from a blast—this one stronger than those caused by disruptor fire. A photon torpedo, Picard decided, even as Data reported:

"Aft shields are down to forty percent."

"Keep our bow to the *Scimitar*," Riker told the helm. "Auxiliary power to the forward shields."

Aboard the *Scimitar*, Shinzon had grown calm and focused during the attack. He had only enough strength to direct his attention to the battle, and nothing else; but he was, after all, a Picard. Tactics came naturally to him.

The fact that the Romulans (at least, Suran and Donatra, if not the entire fleet) had betrayed him surprised him not at all. He had considered the possibility after his last conversation with Suran. But he had not considered that their attack might come during his final battle with Picard.

It mattered not. Shinzon shared the same indomitable spirit as his current prey: and no matter how many obstacles appeared—his rapid degeneration toward death, Picard's escape, the rebellion of the Romulan fleet leader—he would not surrender, would not be overwhelmed. He would rely on his instincts to find solutions.

Shinzon's one great mistake was in believing his tenacity sprang from hatred.

He sat quietly now and issued an order that would bring death to hundreds. They were, after all, only Romulans.

"Target the flanking warbird, all forward disruptor banks on my mark."

He watched as the *Enterprise* and the Romulan vessels continued their relentless firing, all while performing an intricate, fast-moving ballet as ship swept past ship in an apparently random pattern.

Shinzon closed his eyes only briefly—the display of searing lights had left him with a viselike headache. When he opened them again, the blasts had not ceased, nor had the weaving dance of vessels.

"Fire," he said.

He watched with pleasure as the *Scimitar* released a devastating volley of disruptor fire, all forward banks firing at once.

One of the warbirds was fully engulfed in a blazing glow, for a millisecond suspended motionless in the brilliance of death.

And then the hull split neatly apart as the ship was riven down the middle, exposing decks and debris in a fiery explosion. Dozens of tiny bodies hurtled unprotected into space, accompanied by bright red shrapnel that quickly dimmed in the airless void.

Great chunks of twisted metal struck the *Enterprise*'s bow with violent force.

In his command chair, Shinzon smiled.

• • •

The *Enterprise* recoiled as pieces of the destroyed warbird slammed into its hull.

"Forward shields are down to ten percent," Data called over the noise.

"Bring us about!" Riker ordered the helm.

The explosion had happened so quickly that Picard had not had the time to determine whether the valiant Commander Donatra's vessel was the one destroyed; either way, he deeply regretted the destruction.

The captain kept a hand on the arm of his chair as the *Enterprise* arced about, firing her aft phasers. Meanwhile, the remaining warbird bore down on the *Scimitar* and continued to fire her disruptors.

Shinzon watched as, on the viewscreen, the *Valdore* approached. Donatra's defection troubled him more than Suran's; perhaps because she was younger and more open to change, and he had trusted her to be loyal. The notion came to him that she had been possessed of an uncommon self-honesty and nobility—but he quickly squelched the thought. Impossible, that he should find any Romulan likeable.

The viceroy turned expectantly to Shinzon, awaiting the order to destroy a second vessel.

"Let her pursue," Shinzon said. "Drop cloak on the aft port quadrant—and prepare for full emergency stop."

Vkruk was so startled that, for the first time, he questioned one of his praetor's orders. "What?"

Shinzon's tone grew sharp; time was too valuable. "You heard me."

• • •

On the *Valdore,* Donatra kept her thoughts on the battle; grief would have to wait for another time—though watching the annihilation of Suran's ship left her numbed, empty, much as she had felt as a girl after they had taken her father away. She would take time to reflect on her mentor, she promised herself; she would deal with her guilt at not speaking out against Shinzon sooner . . . But she could rest easy in that knowledge that Suran had ultimately made the right choice, had died an honorable death.

Her best course of action now was to avenge him. And as the *Valdore* hurtled in pursuit of the praetor, Donatra watched as, on the viewscreen, a section of the *Scimitar*'s hull flickered into view.

"He's losing his cloak!" she shouted to her tactical officer. "Stand by all forward disruptor banks!"

"She almost on us . . ." the viceroy reported.

Shinzon heard the hint of anxiety in the Reman's tone; he also sensed the growing restlessness in his bridge crew. The praetor was continuing to age, and knew it was reflected in his physical features. Perhaps even Vkruk was worried that his master was losing his mental capacity as well, and was unfit for command.

No matter, Shinzon told himself; he would prove himself well enough in the next few seconds. He ignored the nervous glances directed at him and said, "Not yet . . ."

The *Valdore* flew perilously close to the *Scimitar;* at this range, a disruptor blast at the uncloaked hull could cause serious damage.

"Praetor..." the viceroy began to complain, but his reproach was drowned out by Shinzon's emphatic command.

"FULL STOP AND FIRE!"

His officers, finally understanding, obeyed.

Shinzon was thrown back against his chair as his ship came to an abrupt halt in space—too fast for the *Valdore* to respond. She went sailing harmlessly over the Reman vessel—

And the *Scimitar* fired a full volley of photon torpedoes into her belly and aft as she streaked past.

A deep roar vibrated in Donatra's eardrums, in her jaw, in her very bones. Blinded by searing brightness, she went flying from the confines of her chair. She struck other objects: hard things, whether bulkheads or consoles or chairs, she could not say; and softer, more yielding objects—bodies.

For seconds, she could not orient herself, could feel nothing but pain. And then she forced her eyes open and tried to push herself to a sitting position. Her first effort failed—apparently her wrist had been broken, but she used one elbow and the opposite hand to finally sit up.

Visibility was limited by smoke and darkness; she drew in a breath and coughed at the unnatural stench of consoles and circuitry afire. But she could see well enough to discover that she had been thrown against the console and chair of the communications officer. A further scan revealed the body of the officer, Venar, lying only an arm's reach from her; she reached forth, gave Venar's elbow a gentle shake, then recoiled when the man's head lolled toward her at an unnatural angle, revealing open, lifeless eyes.

Carefully, wincing at ribs either bruised or broken, Donatra rolled onto her knees and caught hold of the edge of the chair. After a time, she managed to pull herself onto unsteady feet.

"Report," she ordered sternly.

No reply came. Gingerly, she made her way across the dark, smoke-filled bridge, lit only by the sparks that occasionally sputtered from damaged equipment. She knew her vessel well: and though the viewscreen had gone dark, she sensed that the *Valdore* was no longer moving, but floating helplessly in space. The hum of the warp engines had ceased altogether.

On her way to her command chair, she literally stumbled over the bodies of her helm officer, a promising young woman named Tvana, and her second-in-command, Tolan. Surprise made her cry out: but when she gathered herself, her upper body lying across the male, her lower across the female, she rolled to one side and checked each officer for signs of life.

There were none; she, Donatra, was the only one alive on her bridge. She pressed a slightly trembling hand to her forehead and frowned at the bloodied palm that came away.

At the same time on the *Scimitar* bridge, Shinzon watched, gloating, as the second warbird careened helplessly into space, then glided, powerless and dark, to a stop. Donatra could betray him no longer.

In the off-chance she was still alive, he considered blowing the *Valdore* to bits, ensuring that there would be no survivors; but he could spare neither the power nor the time.

Donatra was no longer a threat to him; Picard was.

The hour had come for Shinzon to take Picard, to use the captain's life to fuel his own. There could be no more empathy, no more admiration, no more delays.

"Restore the aft cloak and bring us about," Shinzon told his viceroy and the helmsman.

They obeyed without hesitation: They had learned not to question their praetor, even in his moments of physical weakness.

Shinzon settled back with an exhausted sigh, thinking only of the blood that would bring him strength.

The *Enterprise* viewscreen showed a dismaying sight: Commander Donatra, leaning heavily against her communications console, her dark hair tousled, her face smudged with soot. Rivulets of dark emerald blood streaked her brow and one cheek.

Behind her lay smoke-enshrouded ruins; the unmanned helm was a mangled mass of metal sparks; the bridge was in darkness except for the faint red glow of emergency lighting.

Even so, Picard could make out the silhouette of bodies strewn across the deck. An image of the *Enterprise* bridge and its crew in similar circumstances flashed in his mind. He repressed it firmly.

Donatra spoke, her voice much fainter this time. "I'm afraid that drink will have to wait, Captain."

"Do you have life support?" Picard asked. He could not help but sympathize with her unexpressed grief: she was in the one situation no commander ever wants to face: survival, when one's crew is killed.

"For the moment," Donatra said, with the slight hitching of breath that indicated broken ribs. "But we're dead in the water."

"Understood—" Picard began, then was hurled to one side as the *Enterprise* pitched under a fresh attack.

Picard fought for purchase, head reeling as the deck rolled beneath him. This time, the thunder of disruptor blasts was accompanied by the shriek of metal. The *Enterprise* herself groaned and shuddered as she was torn apart; the roaring in Picard's ears deafened him to all else, and the ship's throes caused his teeth to vibrate in his jaw.

After a swift eternity, he managed to catch hold of his console arm, to right himself, but the ship was still listing. She had suffered structural damage, Picard knew, even before the roaring ceased and his inner ears once again oriented him to up and down, front and back.

Data reported, his voice finally audible. "We have lost structural integrity on decks twelve through seventeen, sections four through ten.

Geordi followed. "Emergency force fields are holding."

"Evacuate those decks and reroute field power to forward shields," Riker ordered.

It was Deanna Troi who went to Picard; Deanna who made the offer he could never ask of her, though he had called her to the bridge, counting on her to make the right decision when the circumstances demanded it. He looked on her with both pride and reluctance as she spoke.

"Captain—I might have a way to find them."

"Counselor?" he asked gently, though he already knew the answer.

She squared her shoulders; in her black eyes shone no fear, only determination. "The one thing he may have forgotten in the course of battle: me."

"Make it so," Picard said, grateful.

She moved swiftly to Worf at tactical.

• • •

On the *Scimitar,* Shinzon entered strategic commands in his chair console; at the same time, he gave orders to the viceroy that would ensure the *Enterprise*'s crippling but Picard's survival.

"Prepare a lateral run—all starboard disruptors."

Shinzon continued to enter commands, confident his second-in-command would obey. But in his peripheral vision, he saw Vkruk stiffen, saw the Reman's expression grow slack with panic as his gaze focused inward . . .

"No . . ." the Viceroy whispered.

At tactical, Deanna Troi stood beside Worf, her small, pale hand moving the Klingon's large bronze one over the photon torpedo targeting display.

Her eyes were closed, her breath intentionally slow and steady as she struggled to shut out all distractions: the sights and sounds of the bridge in battle, of her own fears that she and Will would never set sail on the Opal Sea, that her crewmates would soon be killed, that the captain would die at Shinzon's hands.

But the worst fear of all overtook her when she mentally summoned up the image of the viceroy: that of experiencing further violation of her most private self—her mind.

She calmed at once and instead focused on his image: on his great, skeletal head with its bone-white promontories and shadowed recesses, its jutting lower jaw with sharpened teeth, its deeply inset eyes incapable of shining with compassion or respect for any being who was not Reman or the prophesied Shinzon.

She calmed, and saw the Reman where he stood: on the bridge beside his aging praetor. On the *Scimitar* bridge, dressed in his tunic that shone like an insect's hard carapace, black shot through with glints of purple, his white face reflecting the malachite-green glow of a console display.

He sensed her. His revulsion at her touch, his own fear, passed through her like a shudder; she grimaced with the agony of it.

"He's resisting me—" Deanna murmured to the captain, but she had no doubt the viceroy heard her as well. She felt, she saw, the Reman concentrate, rejecting the contact. In her mind, she heard ghostly whispers.

Shinzon's voice: *What is it?!*

The viceroy—no, Vkruk. His real name was Vkruk: *She is here.*

On the *Enterprise* bridge, Deanna's body flushed with sudden heat as the intensity of her focus increased. Her breath quickened; she could feel beads of perspiration moisten her forehead, her palm pressed against the back of Worf's hand as she continued to move it over the targeting display.

At the same time, she saw Vkruk, his features taut, his teeth bared with the effort of resistance: and then his image faded, replaced by that of the *Scimitar*'s bridge. She stood beside the praetor—beside Shinzon, sitting bent and wizened like an old man, the veins on his face, his bare scalp, standing in bas relief. She saw the console display, its glow green on her face.

She was in the Reman's mind. Swiftly, she used Vkruk's knowledge to read the tactical display, to locate the precise coordinates of the *Scimitar*.

The Reman sensed the violation: with horror, he mentally

recoiled from her, and in her mind's eye, Deanna once again saw his image. This time she glared at him fearlessly.

Remember me?

At once, Deanna severed the connection. On the *Enterprise* bridge, she snapped open her eyes as she pulled Worf's hand to the exact spot, then cried: "NOW!"

Worf pressed the control, instantly firing a full spread of photon torpedoes.

Deanna held her breath.

Against the turbulent backdrop of the Bassen Rift's lightninglike bolts of energy, the first torpedo connected with the *Scimitar*'s shields, illuminating for an instant the outline of the predator ship.

And then another torpedo hit its mark; and another, and another, and another, until the glowing shields flickered, then faded, revealing the *Scimitar* herself, uncloaked at last.

Picard rose, swift and straight, from his chair. "Fire at will!"

Deanna watched as Worf's strong hands moved quickly over the tactical controls, firing all phasers, all photon torpedoes.

A millisecond later, on the screen, the *Scimitar* was struck by the devastating attack.

It would have destroyed a weaker vessel. Yet the *Scimitar* sped out of the line of fire and herself unleashed a deadly volley.

But she had paid a price. Shinzon looked about his bridge and for the first time, experienced acute desperation. On the deck before him lay a large piece of railing from the upper deck; the attack had turned it into shrapnel. It had hurtled down, barely grazing the top of Shinzon's head. A mere finger's breadth lower, and it might well have decapitated him. As it was, it lay with other pieces of debris torn loose by the *Enterprise*'s phasers; everywhere Shinzon looked, he saw damaged consoles sputtering green sparks.

It finally occurred to Shinzon that Picard, though raised in a gentle culture and possessed of pacifistic beliefs, was—if provoked to self-defense—every bit as cunning as his clone, every bit as determined, every bit as deadly.

Perhaps, Shinzon thought with a pang of fear, the captain's years of experience in real battles made him even more so— and the one called praetor entertained another new concept: that Picard might actually win.

Shinzon forced himself to abandon such thinking, but the ever-mounting desperation remained. He spun to face his viceroy.

"Prepare a boarding party—BRING ME PICARD!"

As the viceroy strode off to fulfill orders, Shinzon addressed his helm and tactical officers.

"Get the cloak back! And target shield coordinates beta-three. All disruptors. Fire!"

The *Enterprise* bridge rocked.

"Captain," Data reported, ever calm in the face of emergency, "we have lost ventral shielding on deck twenty-nine."

"Divert power and compensate—"

Picard's words were drowned out by the harsh shriek of an alarm Klaxon.

Worf straightened at once. "Intruder alert!"

The captain did not ask why the intruders had come; he already knew. He glanced at Riker.

"Let's go," Riker said to Worf, and he and the Klingon headed for the turbolift as the Klingon pressed his combadge.

"Security detail to deck twenty-nine."

Data moved at once to Worf's position at tactical.

The lower decks of the *Enterprise* were dimly lit to reflect night; as red alarm lights strobed eerily in the corridors, Riker and Worf led a security contingent in search of the intruders. They walked in taut silence, weapons at the ready: Riker was content with a standard issue phaser, while Worf and some of his detail had armed themselves with rifles.

It was obvious to Will that the Remans had come for Picard, and for that reason, he would do whatever was necessary— sacrifice himself, if need be—to protect the captain. But Will had another good reason to stop the invaders—a reason that had nothing to do with his officer's training or his loyalty to Picard, and everything to do with Deanna.

Any group that thought nothing of mentally abusing another had to be stopped—and Riker was eager to volunteer for the job.

As they proceeded cautiously through the corridors, Worf finally spoke quietly to Riker, so softly that the others did not hear. "The Romulans . . . fought with honor," the Klingon said, giving Riker a sidewise glance.

The profundity of the statement did not escape Riker. For Worf to admit that a Romulan was capable of any worthy act marked a true shift in the Klingon's belief system. The Romulans' willingness to sacrifice themselves in order to stop Shinzon had clearly opened Worf's mind and emotions, had allowed him to see that Romulan individuals were responsible for the brutal deaths of his parents at Khitomer. Individuals, and not an entire race.

"They did, Mister Worf," Will replied slowly, taking the lesson to heart.

The Reman who had attacked Deanna did not represent all Remans; perhaps others of his race found his actions as despicable as Riker did. At any rate, Will struggled not to judge.

Self-defense against those who wished Earth harm was, of course, another matter . . .

A blinding disruptor blast stopped Will's train of thought. It ricocheted off the bulkhead, leaving behind the smell of scorched metal.

At the far end of the corridor stood the intruders, perhaps a dozen Remans—led by the one Will instantly recognized as the viceroy.

The one, Riker knew, who had assaulted his wife. He struggled less than a second to contain his hatred—then allowed himself to feel it, to allow the attendant adrenaline to help him in battle.

He and the other security crew members returned fire, lighting up the corridor in a dazzling display. The light apparently hurt the Remans' eyes, for they all grimaced; some raised their free hands as shields.

The *Enterprise* crew continued firing until the Remans retreated slightly, but they continued to answer with disruptor blasts. Fearless, firing his rifle, Worf led his officers forward as he evaded the Reman blasts skillfully.

The *Enterprise* group was gaining the upper hand easily— too easily, Riker decided. Perhaps the disruptor fire was actually intended as a distraction . . .

And then he saw it: the viceroy, diving into the nearest Jefferies tube. So that was the plan—to sacrifice the others in a mock battle while one Reman crawled up to the bridge, and the captain.

"Worf!" Riker shouted, pointing at the disappearing viceroy with his chin.

The Klingon followed Riker's gaze and understood instantly. In an amazing acrobatic display, Worf dove headfirst into the corridor, landing on his stomach and sliding forward on the deck beneath the steady stream of disruptor blasts; all the while, the Klingon fired a continuous barrage from his phaser rifle.

It provided the necessary cover for Riker to leap into the Jefferies tube—into the darkness, in pursuit of the viceroy.

Chapter 9

Back on the *Enterprise* bridge, Picard stared tensely at the viewscreen as the *Scimitar* responded to the last attack. The Reman vessel sailed directly at the *Enterprise*'s bow—perilously close.

Picard saw the brilliant glow of photon torpedoes filling the entire screen like blazing novae, and opened his mouth to demand evasive maneuvers—

Too late.

Overhead, the bridge hull was sheared away with a force that vibrated in the very core of Picard's being; it lifted him straight from his chair then crushed him hard against it, as if he had collided with a sun.

The radiance left him momentarily blinded. When his sight cleared, he saw the viewscreen and part of the forward bridge explode into glittering shards and go flying out into space. In the instant before the emergency force field took hold, he felt the air sucked from his lungs, felt the pull of space's intense vacuum and held fast to his chair; and in that same horrifying millisecond, the young ensign was wrenched up from the helm, turned onto his side and hurtled upward, outward in a gruesome parody of an antigrav exercise—out into the airless void, to his death.

The sight tore at Picard's heart—the ensign was young, unseasoned, excited about his recent assignment to the *Enterprise*—but for the sake of the others, now was not the time to grieve.

The fields took hold; the pull of space eased, oxygen returned, and Picard's lungs refilled themselves with an audible gasp. As Deanna raced to take the helm, the captain stared through the gaping wound in the bridge hull. Just beyond, the *Scimitar* was banking for another attack run.

Suddenly, an aft section of the Reman ship disappeared.

"He's getting his cloak back," Geordi said.

Data followed with more dismal information. "We have exhausted our compliment of photon torpedoes. Phaser banks are down to four percent."

"What if we target all phasers in a concentrated attack?" If, Picard reasoned, they could cripple the *Scimitar*'s warp drive, her deadliness would be limited to the Bassen Rift.

But Data shook his head. "The *Scimitar*'s shields are still at seventy percent. It would make no difference, sir."

Picard thought. No solution presented itself immediately, but he would find one. Shinzon had expected an easy win, and thus far, Picard had made things extraordinarily difficult for him.

And the captain intended to present him with even greater difficulties, and no win at all.

"They're stopping . . ." Deanna said.

Picard glanced back through the hole in his bridge and watched as the *Scimitar* slowly turned, then began to advance. Another section of its hull flickered, then disappeared beneath the cloak.

"What's he doing?" Geordi wondered aloud.

Picard's tone was grim; he understood the maneuver, for it was one the darkest part of his soul would desire before confronting an enemy in a hopeless situation. "He wants to look me in the eye."

In the darkness of the labyrinth, Riker stalked the viceroy.

It was not the most ideal situation for a human hunting a Reman. The access tunnels were draped in shadow— *dark as Remus*, Will thought—illuminated only by the pulsating red alarm strobes. The viceroy would have perfect sight under such conditions; Riker, on the other hand, had to strain to see.

Yet he had an advantage the Reman did not: a fury and determination born of his love for Deanna. It mattered not whether the Reman was physically stronger, or telepathic, or able to see in the dark. For Deanna's sake—as well as the sake of his captain and crew—Riker would win.

But as he moved stealthily through the tunnels, Riker grew increasingly tense. He tightened his grip on the phaser in his hand and looked slowly, carefully, in front and behind him: Only the occasional red flashes allowed him to see.

In either direction, the tunnels were empty.

But the thrill in the pit of Riker's stomach said he was not alone: He had the distinct sensation that he was being watched. He stopped, squinting at the darkness ahead and raised his phaser to eye level—the level of a Reman chest.

A flash of reflective purplish black, the white gleam of bone: Instinctively, Riker glanced upward just as the Reman let go of the skeletal framework overhead and came flying down at him.

Body struck body. Riker dropped to his knees as his phaser was knocked away and went skittering across the deck. The alarm light pulsed again, and in its crimson glow, he saw the dully gleaming metal of a Reman dagger, heard it whistle through the air as it came arcing down toward him.

Picard stood and looked beyond the flickering field that protected him and his remaining bridge crew from suffocation and the energy pulses of the Bassen Rift, at the *Scimitar* as it prepared for its final run.

Only a few hundred yards from the *Enterprise,* the mighty warbird stopped, its bow just shy of the bridge's force field.

The captain's mind raced. He knew, of course, that Shinzon would now demand that Picard turn himself over if he wanted to save his ship.

At the same time, Picard knew Shinzon's word could not be trusted. Out of pure revenge, Shinzon would destroy the *Enterprise;* he had no reason now to spare her, and every reason to seek revenge on his double.

Yet Shinzon was counting on the captain as having no choice—for if Picard refused, he and his ship would surely be destroyed. If he gave himself over to Shinzon, if he, in his last moments, could appeal to Shinzon's humanity to save the *Enterprise,* then perhaps . . .

That, Picard knew, was Shinzon's reasoning—and so he, Picard, had to think of the opposite of his natural inclination.

And his natural inclination was to protect his ship and crew at any cost.

"*We've got him,*" Picard exulted. He sat in his chair and began punching commands into his console.

Geordi gazed quizzically at him with pale eyes. "Sir. . . ?"

Picard did not quite smile. "He thinks he knows exactly what I'm going to do . . ."

And on the *Scimitar* bridge, Shinzon thought precisely that. His desperation had subsided; now that the battle was his, he decided that he was, in fact, deeply grateful to Picard for putting up such a valiant effort—for it showed what he, Shinzon, was made of. Had his double been any less difficult to capture, Shinzon would not have known the true depths of his own resiliency.

At the same time, the difficulty *had* angered and frustrated Shinzon to the point that he hated Picard while still admiring him.

Time now for Picard to play the role he'd spent his whole life preparing for: that of the noble martyr.

Smug, Shinzon settled back into his chair. "Open a channel."

While Picard was still busily entering commands in his console, Data reported, "We are being hailed."

Picard stayed focused on his work, but spoke to Troi at the helm. "Deanna, stand by . . ." The captain then glanced over at Data. "Open a channel."

Out of habit, Picard looked briefly up at the force field where the viewscreen had been, where the *Scimitar*—at least, what was still visible of her—loomed.

Shinzon's disembodied voice, filled with gloating, filtered over the comm. "I hope you're still alive, Jean-Luc."

"I am." Picard returned to his work of punching in commands.

"Don't you think it's time to surrender? Why should the rest of your crew have to die?"

Unmoved, Picard finished his work, then transmitted the codes to Deanna at the helm. She received them and understood them—he could tell by the slight stiffening of her posture—but otherwise, she showed no fear. She simply nodded, an officer bravely carrying out her duty.

Picard stalled for time, saying easily to Shinzon, "I never told you about my first Academy evaluation, did I? I received very high marks for my studies. But I was found lacking in certain other areas. Personality traits, you might say. In particular, I was thought to be extremely . . ." He glared up at the *Scimitar*'s bow, "over-confident."

"Captain," Shinzon said dryly, "as much as I enjoy listening to you talk—"

Picard gestured swiftly for Data to sever the comm link, then ordered, "Geordi, put *all power* to the engines—take it from life support if you have to—everything you can give me."

"Aye, sir."

"Deanna, on my mark."

"Ready, sir," Geordi advised.

Picard leaned forward and pressed the control that allowed him to be heard by every crew member on the ship: "All hands, brace for impact!" He cut off the link, and told Deanna, "ENGAGE."

• • •

Aghast and disbelieving, Shinzon bolted straight up from his chair at the sight of the impossible: the crippled, scorched *Enterprise,* using what surely was her last surge of power, headed on a direct collision course with the *Scimitar.* In the instant it took Shinzon to realize this, his commander's instinct told him that, on her current course, the Federation captain would lay waste to his bridge—and worse, his engines.

Picard is mad, Shinzon thought, even as he shouted aloud: "HARD TO PORT!"

He could easily imagine Picard sacrificing himself; but it seemed unthinkable that a human who possessed such a soft philosophy would also allow the sacrifice of his crew. It never occurred to Shinzon that such weak creatures as the other humans aboard the *Enterprise* might share the same sentiment as his Reman crew: a willingness to sacrifice themselves for their captain, for the greater good.

The *Scimitar* banked sharply, but not soon enough.

The squeal and groan of metal crushing metal assaulted Shinzon first, piercing his skull as the battered *Enterprise* bridge appeared on the viewscreen; through its large gap, he saw Picard in his chair—and then Shinzon went flying out of his own.

Chaos. Brilliant blue-green lights, the blur of metal raining down onto the lower bridge, bodies tumbling down from above, the enraged death-screams of warriors.

Shinzon collided hard against something muscular, solid, with a dull crunch; he gasped at the sensation of his now-brittle ribs cracking.

The deck still rocked, but he pushed himself up—and saw that beneath him lay the body of his tactical officer.

"Get up," Shinzon ordered, himself managing to struggle to his knees, despite the catch in his ribs.

But the Reman remained facedown, motionless. With a swift move, Shinzon reached beneath the officer's chin and turned the Reman's face toward him—only to find that the front of the Reman's domed forehead had been crushed inward, the result of a collision with his console.

Shinzon let the officer's chin drop; the head lolled to one side. Shaking with hatred and weakness, Shinzon pushed himself to his feet. The *Scimitar*'s once-elegant bridge was nothing now but a mass of twisted metal and darkened, sputtering consoles. Of the dozen officers who had manned it, only two now struggled to rise.

Picard would now die, Shinzon swore to himself. Whether he, Shinzon, survived was immaterial. No matter the cost, Picard would now die.

And through the gaping wound in his own bridge, Picard clutched his chair just long enough to see the *Enterprise*'s forward saucer smash its way into the *Scimitar*'s shuttlebay, and tear through a row of *Scorpion* fliers.

As he, too, was hurled from his chair, Picard fought a deep sense of disappointment. He had hoped to see the *Scimitar*'s engineering decks, had hoped to see her warp core flicker and go dark. He had to do far more than impose structural damage on Shinzon's vessel—or he would be called upon to make the greatest sacrifice of all.

Seconds earlier, Worf had been crawling on his belly on deck twenty-nine, firing a constant barrage of rifle blasts as

Riker escaped into the Jefferies tube after the viceroy. The cover provided by the security personnel behind the Klingon permitted him to successfully stun two of the Remans; a Terran female lieutenant, Chin, stunned a third.

Worf tried to use the cover of the others' fire to scramble to his feet—but before he could do so, a burst of disruptor fire struck the bulkhead just beside him, so close that the skin on his back tingled as if with an electrical shock. The intense blaze left an afterimage in the center of his vision.

At once, his people moved forward, forcing the Remans back; Chin hurried forward and gathered up disruptors from the fallen Remans.

As Worf got to his feet, the Remans retreated further—as if intentionally drawing the *Enterprise* detail onward. At the next juncture of corridors, the group parted; five of the Remans headed in one direction, three in another. Worf gave Chin, next in command, a quick nod. Understanding, she led all but one other security officer, the young Ensign Mbewa, after the five Remans; Worf and Mbewa continued after the remaining three.

By that time, the three Remans had disappeared around a curve in the corridor; Worf and Mbewa approached cautiously, rifles raised—but even they, with all their speed, were no match for the swiftness of the assault awaiting them.

The instant they rounded the corridor, they were met—not with disruptor fire, but with two of the Remans leaping forward at them, large, ugly daggers raised. The Remans' height gave them an advantage: focused on firing straight ahead, Worf did not expect an attack coming directly from above, and so he was caught off guard by the aliens' swiftness.

Mbewa, young and not so experienced, cried out as the dagger plunged into the juncture of his neck and shoulder; his attacker used the opportunity to strip away his phaser rifle. But Mbewa pulled back, knife still firmly planted in his body, and prepared for hand-to-hand combat.

Meanwhile, the Klingon, whose strength was a better match for the Remans, lifted his phaser rifle just in time for his own attacker's dagger to hit the rifle with a loud ring of metal. Using the rifle as a shield, Worf battered the Reman, finally knocking him unconscious with a strong blow to the chin.

Then the Klingon turned, remembering the existence of the third Reman an instant too late: the pale, gaunt-looking giant was waiting at the corridor's end, disruptor already aimed and ready to fire.

"No!" Worf shouted, and fired his own rifle in reply.

The blast stunned the third Reman, enveloping the outline of his body for a dazzling millisecond before he fell—but not before the blast from his disruptor found his target: Ensign Mbewa. In the second before his death, the young human writhed, caught in the bright, fatal energy surge, and cried out in pain.

And then his body vaporized—incinerated so completely, not even ash remained.

The Klingon roared with pure fury, and turned to stun the remaining Reman—who, despite his height, ran with impossible swiftness down the corridor. But Worf was, at this moment, also capable of the impossible: so he followed, stride for stride, as the Reman fled for cover, who had abandoned his knife in favor of his disruptor, and now occasionally turned to fire over his shoulder.

Worf did not attempt to avoid the blasts: He felt no fear, only a determination so strong that he knew the Reman was his. Nor did he bother to fire, for such only slowed him down, and his aim was sure to prove inaccurate. Instead, he gained ground steadily on the Reman until the alien, realizing that he was about to be captured, fled into the nearest doorway—the one leading to the cargo bay.

At the instant he entered, the ship suddenly lurched; the deck beneath Worf's feet gave way, and he was thrown hard against the open doorway. The ship echoed with the grinding sound of metal against metal . . . The two ships, Worf realized, with great admiration for Picard's courage, were locked together in a death-battle.

But the Klingon would not permit the shuddering deck to stop him from pursuing his own battle to the death. Worf recovered his balance and ran inside—and was at once disturbed to see that the bay had been converted into a triage area; obviously, Dr. Crusher, who was helping to move a patient to an antigrav gurney, no longer had enough room in sickbay to handle all the wounded.

Before the Reman could move near the patients or the medical personnel, Worf fired at him—but the blast only caught the edge of his hand, knocking his disruptor away. Worf moved forward for better aim, but the Reman was too swift; he seized the nearest medic—the one who had just helped Dr. Crusher—and took his phaser, firing back at Worf. With a sweeping motion of his arm, the Reman knocked both humans to the floor with near-deadly force.

Crouching beside a wounded patient for cover, the alien fired the hand phaser—then, realizing from its harmless ricochet off the bulkhead that it was set only for stun, reset it at once to kill, dissolving the medical equipment next to Worf.

For an instant, no more, the Klingon hesitated. He could follow the Reman into the maze of the wounded and the medics trying to treat them—or he could offer himself as a moving target, hoping that the distraction would allow one of the armed personnel to capture the Reman.

And so he ran around the periphery of the triage area in random fashion, drawing the Reman's fire—and barely avoiding being shot. One disruptor blast, close enough to raise the hairs on his scalp; two. The Reman stayed in his protected area, as close to the wounded patient as possible. In frustration, Worf stopped, stood spreadeagle, and cried out:

"You fight with no honor!"

The temptation for the Reman was too great; with a grimace that was apparently a smile, he half rose beside the gurney and took deliberate aim, firing with deadly accuracy.

At the last moment, Worf moved; but not enough. The killing phaser beam caught his arm, his shoulder, filled his eyes with a burning brilliance that allowed no other sight, no other sensation, no other sound. For that blazing instant, he knew only light; and in the next, only darkness.

What Worf did not see, did not know, was that in the time he was partially caught in the phaser beam, Beverly Crusher rose, a look of grim determination on her features, and brought down the Reman with a neatly aimed stun beam.

Just as quickly, she threw the phaser aside and ran to where the Klingon lay, the uniform and top layers of skin completely burned away from his arm and shoulder. She quickly ran a hand scanner over him.

"Worf, dear God . . ."

The skin could be easily regenerated; but his heart tissue had been severely damaged, and he was in the final stages of arrest. Crusher yelled over her shoulder at no one in particular.

"Get me a gurney and a regenerative defibrillator—STAT!"

In the Jefferies tube, Riker had just enough time to see the Reman blade come hurtling toward him and to catch the Reman's wrist before the two of them were slammed violently against the bulkheads.

The knife went rattling across the deck; both men fought for footing, but the *Enterprise* shuddered so violently that for an instant, neither could rise. There came an intense sensation of impact such as Riker had never felt, followed by an ear-splitting screech—metal on metal, Riker decided, and realized with a sense of wonder that the two ships were colliding.

But Will could not spare his concentration: He focused on the Reman, who was crawling toward the knife. Riker leapt upon the Reman—and again, the ship lurched, causing the two to be slammed together. Riker took advantage of the situation and got his hands around his enemy's throat.

The Reman's eyes were dark, darker than Deanna's, yet each time the red strobes flashed, Riker could catch a glimpse of its slitted pupils contracting, deeper black against black. The flesh against Riker's palms felt cool and reptilian to the touch; beneath it were muscles so thick and strong that Riker could feel no bones, no larynx, no cords. He applied all of his strength—yet the Reman did not gasp, did not struggle for air, merely clutched Riker's wrists and with inexorable strength, pried them away from his throat.

Physically, Will realized, there was no way he could win— no more than the *Enterprise,* pitted weapon for weapon, could prevail against the *Scimitar.* Strategy was called for.

But as the viceroy succeeded in prying Riker's hands apart and in turn placed his spindly but crushingly strong claws around the human's neck, strategy seemed frighteningly distant.

On his ruined bridge, Shinzon stood amidst the smoke and bodies and watched the scene on one of the few working monitors, that of the two ships locked together, the *Enterprise*'s saucer wedged firmly into the *Scimitar*'s flank.

Tactical had gone dark, but the helm was working, and one of the two surviving bridge officers hurried to man it.

"Divert all power to the engines," Shinzon called to him. "Full reverse!"

Shinzon braced himself as the deck began to tremble.

As the *Scimitar* slowly began to tear herself free, the *Enterprise* was thrashed from side to side. Metal shrieked as it was ripped apart: Even deep within the Federation ship's belly, the sound vibrated in Riker's jaw and teeth. The first jolt threw the viceroy backward, causing his keen-edged talons to scrape the skin from Riker's neck. The Reman recovered his footing just as Riker scrambled to his own feet; Riker staggered after him as the two were pitched from bulkhead to bulkhead by the ship's rocking.

The Reman regained full balance first; in a terrible instant, Riker, pinned by gravity against the bulkhead, realized the viceroy was about to spring on him for a final attack. In that same instant, he saw nearby an access plate loosened by the ship's lurches, outlined in the darkness by the brilliant glow of the power relays hidden beneath it.

The Reman coiled.

Riker leaped for the plate and tore it from the bulkhead, unleashing a brilliant flood of light.

The viceroy grimaced with pain and raised clawed hands to his eyes, disoriented; in the brightness, his features looked even more menacing than before. Riker dove for him, slammed into him at waist level . . .

And let go a small cry as they both tumbled down into an apparently depthless vertical access tunnel.

Instinctively, Riker grabbed for the rung he knew had to be there; after an agonizing second of uncertainty, he caught hold.

A stabbing, almost unbearable pain shot through his lower leg, as if he had been pierced with a knife; and then he felt the weight, and looked down.

The Reman clung to him, talons digging deep into the leg of Riker's uniform. He began slowly to climb up the human's body; beyond him lay a fatal drop.

Riker swung out with one hand and, careful to avoid the sharp, gnashing teeth, smashed his palm against the creature's nose and forced its head back.

The Reman fought to press it forward again; using one set of talons like a grappling hook, he swung his other hand upward, seeking purchase in Riker's midback.

Riker shook one leg, forcing the viceroy off balance again; he glared down at his enemy and made himself think of Deanna, sobbing in sickbay as she struggled to speak of what had been done to her; Deanna, recoiling from him in horror as he tried to kiss her; Deanna, her voice breaking as she tried to explain why she had seemed so terrified of the man she loved. Hatred rose in him again; and while it fueled his strength, it was still not enough for what he had to force himself to do.

Riker thought of the beauty of his native Alaska, of untouched snow on the mountains, of ancient evergreens; and he thought of it all, and the people he loved there, dissolved to ash in an instant.

The Reman was inhumanly strong; for the moment, Riker was stronger. He pushed once more against the Reman's face; pushed, and forced its head back so close to a right angle he thought it would snap. Through sheer will, he maintained relentless pressure; and when he felt he could press no more, the viceroy's head went back a bit farther. And then its chest lifted up and away from him; and then its torso reared back.

At last, its claws began to retract, to slip from Riker's leg; and with a final effort, Riker seized the hand and pulled at the talons embedded in his leg.

The viceroy, dangling against the black, apparently bottomless drop, stared up at him in surprise.

Riker stared down at the Reman with disgust. "Don't worry—Hell is dark."

He pushed the white claw away. It flexed once, grasping . . . then spread out in a gesture of succor and helplessness. Riker watched joylessly as his enemy fell silently, inevitably, to his death.

As the *Scimitar* continued to pull herself free, Picard stood, steadying himself on his command chair.

"Data, I need you," he said.

It was not a request he had wanted to make. He had hoped above all to disable the *Scimitar,* to render her navigation or warp drive powerless—but Shinzon had reacted too quickly. Now he was forced to do the one thing he had, as Shinzon had correctly surmised, wanted to avoid at all costs.

Deanna and Will should not be here now, should not be required to make this sacrifice; they should be sailing on the Opal Sea. And Beverly—Beverly should be cutting through the bureaucratic red tape at Starfleet Medical, clucking her tongue over the new medical recruits and their inability to cope with over a hundred different alien anatomies.

Just as the young helmsman should not have died—and all other crew members aboard this vessel should not be having to suffer the same fate.

But Picard knew his regrets were moot; there was no time to make them known—the *Scimitar* was moving away too swiftly. He would do what had to be done: Stop Shinzon from destroying Earth and the Federation.

Data stepped beside his captain as Picard commanded: "Computer. Auto-destruct sequence Omega. Zero time delay. Recognize voice pattern Jean-Luc Picard. Authorization Alpha Alpha Three Zero Five—"

He broke off as the computer droned, "Auto-destruct is off-line."

As if to punctuate his helplessness, the *Enterprise* gave a final lurch: the *Scimitar* was free.

The sudden silence struck Picard as eerie; he watched through the hole in his bridge as the great warbird backed away.

• • •

As Shinzon stared at the image of the battle-scarred *Enterprise,* a wave of dizziness, of pain, of nausea overtook him; so intense were the sensations that he doubled over, and only through a miracle of will managed to stay on his feet. As he slowly straightened, he could feel the very flesh on his face crawling; he was aging, and this time he knew that death was close, very close indeed.

He had heard nothing from the viceroy; and as much as he trusted Vkruk's determination, he felt with a sinking sensation that his friend was forever gone.

Time had run out for them all. He could allow Picard no more time—which meant he could allow himself, Shinzon, no more time, either.

"Target disruptors," he ordered the helm. "Destroy them."

A pause, then the Reman officer reported quietly, "Disruptors are off-line, sir."

Shinzon looked up at the image of the *Enterprise,* and ordered, "Deploy the weapon. Kill everything on that ship. Then set a course for Earth."

The second officer asked swiftly, "What about Picard?"

In his dark eyes, Shinzon detected amazement, concern: How could the mission proceed without the praetor? Gently, he answered, "Our greater goal is more important, brother." He looked back at the image of the wounded *Enterprise.* "Some ideals are worth dying for, aren't they, Jean-Luc?"

The second Reman went to a working console. Soon the entire bridge began to thrum with power as blue-green energy beams coursed upward through the arches of the bridge.

Gasping with effort, Shinzon forced himself up the staircase to the antechamber above. There, a platform in the deck began to fold open: Shinzon watched, mesmerized, as a double-helix energy pulse grew upward, then began to pulse with emerald-green light.

Perhaps it was fitting, he thought, that the weapon he had planned to use against the universe would now be the cause of his own end. Certainly it was fitting that it be Picard's; and Shinzon wondered what his double thought at this very instant, as the *Scimitar* itself began to unfold its deadly array of panels, like a flower in accelerated bloom.

Chapter 10

On the *Enterprise,* Picard and his remaining officers watched as panels began to unfold from the flanks of the *Scimitar.* He, too, was reminded of the image of a flower's petals opening—but his thoughts were far more disciplined than Shinzon gave him credit for.

"How long until he can fire?" Picard asked Geordi.

"The targeting sequence should take about four minutes," the engineer replied, his tone a mix of theoretical fascination and a more practical fatalism.

"But how can he?" Deanna directed her question to the captain. "He'll kill you."

"This isn't about me anymore," Picard answered grimly. He had no more questions, no more strategy; his plan of action had become very simple and direct. He strode to the weapons locker, took a phaser rifle, and ordered Geordi, "Prepare for a site-to-site transport."

La Forge did a split-second double take, caught himself, then said with concern, "Captain, I don't know if the transporter—"

"That's an order, Commander."

"Sir." Data stepped forward. "Allow me to go. You are needed here."

Picard scarcely looked at him. "This is something I have to do."

Deanna took Data's arm. "Let him go."

Picard pressed a control on the rifle; it whined softly as it powered up. To Data, he said, "You have the bridge, Commander. Use all available power to move away from the *Scimitar* . . ." He glanced at Geordi. "Now, Mister La Forge."

"Aye, sir." Clearly nervous, Geordi worked some controls on the console.

Picard saw a shimmer and felt himself begin to dematerialize; he also saw the worried faces of those he cared for gazing on him. As they began to fade and be replaced by the dark architecture of the *Scimitar,* Picard was quite certain this would be the last time he would ever look on them again.

And as Picard finally dematerialized out of view, the transporter panel suddenly sputtered, then exploded in a shower of sparks.

"That's it," Geordi said, hardly believing how calm his own voice sounded, for he was in effect announcing the captain's doom. "Transporters are down."

A moment of terrible silence passed as he, Deanna, and Data exchanged looks. Deanna's was the hardest to bear, for she knew the captain better than any of them. For a moment, Geordi surrendered to a sense of hopelessness; and then Data spoke, with a hint of cheerfulness in his tone that the engineer thought must have been his imagination.

"Counselor Troi, please assume command," the android said politely. "Geordi, if you will come with me."

He headed for the turbolift, Geordi following in wonder.

Aboard the *Scimitar,* Picard materialized in a corridor—one which contained several Reman warriors, their backs to him. They heard the transporter whine and immediately spun about, firing disruptors—but the captain was ready. He crouched instantly and fired in a series of lightning-fast pulses from his rifle.

The Remans fell; Picard moved cautiously on.

On one of the damaged decks, Geordi stood beside Data, staring with him at the end of the corridor, where the vastness of space loomed, thinly veiled by a flickering force field.

In his hands, Geordi held a tricorder, and with the press of a control initiated a separate force field around himself. In the meantime, Data stared out at the distance, and readied himself like an athlete preparing to do the long jump.

"What is our exact distance?" the android asked.

Geordi did a quick scan. "Four hundred thirty-seven meters." It was a wild idea that Data had come up with—so wild that it just might work, and Geordi was willing at this point to do anything that might save the captain and the ship. Data actually managed to make it sound logical.

"Thank you," Data replied, then backed up a little more.

And then he paused, and looked at Geordi a second time— deeply, and Geordi swore to himself that this time it was not his imagination; this time, he clearly saw unmistakable emotion in the android's pale eyes: friendship, and compassion, and true gratitude.

"Thank you, Geordi," Data said simply.

And in that instant, Geordi wanted to remove his force field, to take Data's arm, persuade him not to go—but it was the only chance to save the captain, and besides, it was too late.

Data had already begun to run. He ran down the long corridor with preternatural speed, and when he was but an arm's length from the opening and the field, Geordi pressed a different control on the tricorder. The field snapped off; the vacuum of space rushed in. The violent decompression gave Data momentum as he dove into the rift.

Geordi stayed, watching, a sudden tightness in his throat, a strange emptiness in him, as if his own field had failed and his lungs been sucked empty by the void.

Data floated toward the *Scimitar,* carried by momentum—carried, Geordi realized, too far. As he sailed past the warbird, the android thrust out a hand to catch hold of the ship—and failed, just missing a piece of dangling wreckage.

Helpless, he floated on into space—doomed, Geordi thought with grief. Not only had they lost the captain, but now they had lost Data, and no doubt everyone else aboard the *Enterprise,* too.

Abruptly, Data slammed into something completely invisible and most definitely solid: the cloaked aft of the *Scimitar,* Geordi realized, and grinned broadly. He watched as the android pulled himself onto the invisible hull, ripped open a panel, then climbed slowly inside, disappearing from Geordi's view.

Shinzon stood in the bridge's antechamber, staring into the thalaron activation matrix. The deep emerald glow of the growing energy pulse, as it slowly climbed the double helix, seemed mesmerizing, extraordinarily beautiful.

The sight made him maudlin—or perhaps it was the proximity of death. It was, after all, his legacy to the Reman people, the weapon that would purchase not only their freedom but rulership of the known galaxy. For that, Shinzon was proud; for that, he could die without regret, despite a short and difficult life.

The computer counted down the seconds before the thalaron's deployment. "Fifty-seven . . . Fifty-six . . ."

With some difficulty, Shinzon drew himself away from the jewelike matrix and went down the stairs to the main bridge, where his two officers remained. He stopped before the main screen: there was one more thing he needed to see before he died . . .

The destruction of the *Enterprise*.

He regarded the wounded ship as it floated, helpless, in the rift, its front saucer bearing a long, jagged wound where hull and decks had been torn away, its bridge gaping open. He was only sorry that safety considerations would keep him far enough away so that he could not see Picard die in person.

But Shinzon was able to imagine, as he had upon Praetor Hiren's execution, how death would come for those on the Federation ship, especially Picard. The captain would see the green glow first—and, unlike those in the Romulan Senate Chamber, Picard would be afraid because he would know what followed. The glow would envelop him, caress him, and then his flesh would begin to melt. The pain, Shinzon imagined, would be unspeakable . . .

He was only sorry that the eyes were affected as well, layers of cells sloughing off until blindness resulted. He would have liked Picard to be forced to witness his bridge crew dissolving completely—flesh sloughing off to reveal glistening red muscle, muscle sloughing away to reveal the dissolving internal organs, and bone, and blood . . .

A massive blast behind him interrupted Shinzon's gruesome reverie. He turned, and saw the bridge door exploded inward, and Picard standing in the twisted frame, phaser rifle ready.

There was no time to permit himself to be surprised; Shinzon's first impulse was to protect the thalaron matrix at any cost—a single blast, and the weapon responsible for all his power would be at best crippled, at worst, destroyed. He glanced swiftly at the matrix, tensed as if to move toward it—

Then cursed himself for doing so. Picard caught his look and gesture and understood at once. The captain lifted the rifle and took aim . . .

But the two Remans had already spun about and fired their disruptors. Beams streaked through the air and struck bulkheads as Picard dove for cover behind the remaining railing.

An exchange of fire ensued, lighting up the bridge. Shinzon stared, dazzled and aghast, as Picard first stunned one Reman, then another with astonishing accuracy . . . but a final disruptor blast ricocheted off the bulkhead and grazed his shoulder, knocking the captain to the deck and the phaser rifle from his grasp. It spun away from him as the computer calmly continued the countdown.

". . . Thirty nine . . . Thirty eight . . ."

Utter desperation gave the dying Shinzon a strength he could not possibly have possessed; he sprinted up the stairs toward the antechamber and Picard, at the same time that Picard raced down the stairs for him.

They met halfway. Picard reached for his enemy; Shinzon pulled a jagged-edged dagger from his belt and slashed out at the captain's arms, shoulders, chest. Picard could not win, after all; he had not been tested in the Reman mines in hand-to-hand combat, had not grown up fighting as Shinzon had—

But his jabs met only air as Picard recoiled, smoothly dodging each blow as if he, too, had been born fighting. He caught Shinzon's wrist. To the praetor's surprise, his older double possessed the same strength Shinzon had, before the aging process had begun . . .

Picard gave a hard snap, and the dagger went flying. But Shinzon, dying or not, would not be bested, would not permit himself defeat. Through sheer will, he kicked out; Picard went tumbling, and Shinzon dove into the antechamber, determined to protect it to the end.

Nearby lay a fallen disruptor; Shinzon spotted it, ran for it . . .

At the same time, Picard leaped up and caught a piece of wreckage—a long, jagged section of railing shaken loose during battle. He ran forward to face his enemy, and thrust it forward like a spear . . .

And caught Shinzon in the instant before he could bend down to retrieve the disruptor.

The railing, its edges sharp as any dagger, pierced the younger man just beneath the ribs, just beneath the heart.

Shinzon gazed upon the face of his enemy—so like his own—with infinite disbelief. He, Shinzon, could not lose; he could not be defeated, and certainly it was unthinkable that Picard, of all creatures, should be the one to destroy him.

The disbelief lasted but an instant. In the next, Shinzon accepted that the wound was fatal, that his internal organs were irrevocably damaged, that he would soon die from loss of blood and not from accelerated aging, as he had expected.

But his mind willed that his body would *not* die—not yet, for he was determined to accomplish one grim task before he permitted such an outcome.

The pain was unbearable—yet Shinzon bore it, for he had long ago taught himself to bear the unbearable. Survival was impossible—yet Shinzon prevailed, for he had long ago learned he could accomplish the impossible.

He gritted his teeth, and with a strength his mind, but not his body, possessed, he moved *forward*—toward Picard, forcing the captain back against a bulkhead, forcing his, Shinzon's, body, down the length of the makeshift spear.

The metal crushed its way through his internal organs, pushed itself against the thick muscles and skin of his back—then thrust itself out the other end, glistening with the Praetor's blood. The pain was astounding.

Shinzon grimaced, but made no sound, only continued his inexorable march toward Picard, using the weight of his dying body to pin the captain against the bulkhead. If Shinzon were to die now, he would not permit Picard to live; he would not permit those aboard the *Enterprise* to survive.

He focused on the computer's countdown in an effort to ignore the pain. ". . . Eighteen . . . Seventeen . . ."

"I'm glad we're together now," Shinzon whispered to Picard. "Our destiny is complete."

With agonizing effort, he thrust himself the entire length of the railing and clasped trembling hands around Picard's throat.

• • •

"... Ten ... Nine ..."

Picard heard the seconds tick away with a sense of furious frustration. Shinzon held him pinned in such a manner that, if the captain pushed back against the railing, he would himself be impaled against it. But there had to be a way ... He could not stand helplessly by, bathed in the brilliant green glow of the thalaron activation matrix, and permit his crew, his ship, to be destroyed.

But Shinzon's grip on Picard's neck was alarmingly strong. The captain gagged, but dared not let go of the railing; if it slipped from his grasp, it would pierce through his own chest, just as it had the younger man's. He fought to steer the railing to one side—and succeeded only slightly.

He could only pray Shinzon died before he, Picard, was strangled; and that he was able to maneuver the heavy railing and body away in time to stop the matrix from activating.

Still, Picard struggled.

And as he struggled, he saw, as if in a dream, Data rush into antechamber. Yet it was no dream, no hallucination resulting from wish-fulfillment; the android was real, and without hesitation, he pulled the emergency transport unit from his wrist, and slapped the small silver disk firmly on Picard's shoulder.

Picard was too startled to speak. Nor did Data say a word; he merely gazed on his captain, and in that instant, Picard knew without a doubt that he saw the impossible in eyes supposedly incapable of emotion:

Friendship. Loyalty. Compassion. Nobility. And even—strange as it may seem—happiness, the deep and unalloyed happiness of one who has found deep purpose in life.

Picard parted his lips. There were many things he wanted

to say: first, that Data should not sacrifice himself, that he should destroy the matrix and use the ETU for himself. He was, after all, very near immortal, and his service to Starfleet would continue for centuries, at least—whereas Picard's usefulness was limited to a handful of years. Second, he wanted to say, knowing that Data would refuse to let the captain remain, that he, Picard, was deeply grateful to the android for such a sacrifice; that it had been an honor to know Data, to learn from Data, to have had Data as a friend . . . That he hoped Data knew just how deeply he was esteemed not just by his captain, but by all his friends and crew members aboard the *Enterprise,* and throughout Starfleet.

That he hoped Data knew how much he had changed Picard's life for the better. That he hoped Data knew what a better place the universe was for his having lived in it . . .

But time passed too swiftly for Picard to say any of the thousand things that came to mind. Instead, the computer spoke:

". . . Seven . . . Six . . ."

Data activated the device; the sound of the transporter whined in Picard's ears, and the image of his friend began to fade from view.

Data, still aboard the *Scimitar,* gazed for only an instant at the spot where Picard had stood. He already knew all of the things Picard had not been able to say; he had seen the deep affection and the sorrow in the captain's eyes and had appreciated both.

"Good-bye," he said.

He knew that the captain and the others would miss him very much; he regretted that, but at the same time, he was extremely pleased to be able to save their lives. He thought of Geordi, and the captain, and Deanna and Commander Riker and Dr. Crusher and Worf, and all the other crew members aboard the *Enterprise,* and felt a strange sensation that went beyond pleasure at knowing that he would help them continue to live.

Perhaps this was happiness.

As for his own loss of existence, Data felt no regret. Death held no mystery for him; he had been deactivated before, and knew it was simply nothingness. Unlike a living being, he needed fear no pain. Nor did he have any questions about an afterlife. For him, there could be none.

But there was a fresh meaning given his own life now that he had chosen to limit its span, to be mortal. Captain Picard was right: the awareness of impending death gave life a preciousness, a value it might otherwise not have.

In his final moment, as he pulled out his phaser and fired point-blank into the thalaron matrix, Data allowed himself full access to all memories of his friends simultaneously. And in the glorious instant before the matrix itself exploded in an eruption of emerald and ruby fire, incinerating the android into ash, Data was with all of them.

And as Picard materialized onto the *Enterprise,* he saw, through the gaping hole in his bridge, the brilliant flash as the *Scimitar* dissolved into whirling bits of shrapnel. He did not permit himself to look away, to close his eyes, or to shield them, but permitted himself to be temporarily blinded.

And when the blindness faded, and many of the minute scraps of metal that had been the *Scimitar* had flown away,

Picard continued to stare out through the force field and saw nothing but a faintly glowing field of debris against the darkness of space, illumined erratically by the energy bursts of the Bassen Rift.

He was peripherally aware of Deanna at helm, spinning toward him to search his face, and of Geordi, leaning forward from the upper rear deck, waiting.

Waiting for Data to materialize.

Picard could not speak; but his words would have been wasted, in any regard. Deanna turned back to look at the debris that had been the *Scimitar;* Picard knew from the drop in her shoulders, the sudden stiffening of her posture, that she knew. Nearby, Geordi's head dropped.

Grief settled over Picard, so heavy that he could not move, could only continue to stare beyond the force field at what remained of his friend.

Behind him, the turbolift doors slid open; he heard Riker's voice next to him, asking gently: "Sir?"

Picard could not answer. It was Deanna, skilled in the handling of emotion, who rose and went to her husband. She said but one word.

"Data . . ."

Riker looked out at the glowing ruins of the *Scimitar*. His lips parted slightly, and shock drained all expression from his face. He put an arm around Deanna.

For a long moment, no one spoke.

At last, Geordi announced heavily, "Sir, we're being hailed."

"On screen," Picard responded automatically, then corrected himself as he remembered the screen no longer existed. "Open a channel."

A familiar feminine voice filtered over the comm. "This is Commander Donatra of the *Valdore*. We're dispatching shuttles with medical personnel and supplies."

"Thank you, Commander," Picard said sincerely.

"You've earned a friend in the Romulan Empire today, Captain," Donatra replied. "I hope the first of many. I honor your loss. *Valdore* out."

She severed the link.

"Geordi," Picard said flatly, each word requiring enormous effort. "Prepare the shuttlebay for arrivals. They don't know our procedures so just . . . open the doors."

"I'll take care of it, sir," Geordi replied softly.

"Number One . . ." Picard paused to steady his voice, lest it break. "You have the bridge."

He turned and headed at once for the sanctuary of his ready room, to grieve in private.

When the doors closed over him, Deanna finally allowed herself to cry.

In sickbay, Beverly Crusher was standing over Worf's diagnostic bed with a sense of futility; she had done all she could— the Klingon's shoulder and arm had regenerated nicely, but the damaged area of his heart was not recovering the way it should. It beat arrhythmically when it beat at all, and now he was on life support until Crusher could find the time to research the situation—and pray necrosis of the tissue did not set in.

When she would find that time, she did not know . . . The number of wounded were staggering, and so many of them were priority cases . . .

She raised a hand to her forehead, and rested the other

lightly on Worf's regenerated arm. Her friend was dying, and she did not know what to do to save him.

Behind her, a slightly accented female voice asked, "May I do something to help?"

She turned. If she had not been so battle-weary, so stressed and exhausted, she might have been surprised by who stood behind her: a tall Romulan woman, silver streaks in her dark hair. Unlike every other Romulan Crusher had seen, this one wore not a uniform, but sedate gray civilian dress. Beverly opened her mouth to speak, but found no words.

The Romulan spoke them instead. "I am Doctor Venora, from the *Warbird Valdore*. We have come to provide medical assistance." She lifted a brow ever so slightly as she assessed Beverly's expression, and the hand she had laid on Worf's arm. "He is your friend?"

Beverly nodded. "His heart is damaged . . ."

"And he is experiencing arrhythmia?" Venora asked.

Crusher turned to her, suddenly hopeful.

Chapter 11

In sickbay, Worf woke to find two smiling women standing over him: Dr. Crusher, and, much to his discomfort, a Romulan.

"The Reman . . ." He started, tried to climb off the diagnostic bed, but Crusher genially forced him to remain sitting.

"In the brig with the others. Let me tell you, Commander, you gave me a terrible start—in fact, you almost died. And if you ever decide to pull another stunt like the one you pulled—"

"I do not understand," Worf said, taken aback by the doctor's good-natured scolding.

"Drawing the Reman's fire. Very nearly succeeding in sacrificing yourself. If you ever do that again, Worf, I promise I'll shoot you myself."

Worf grunted, assuming that this was another attempt at Terran humor, which continued to elude him. With dignity, he said, "I am feeling well, now, Doctor, and will return to my post." He rose, and as an afterthought, told her: "Thank you for saving my life."

"I didn't save it," Crusher countered, then gestured at the Romulan woman standing beside her. "Doctor Venora from the *Valdore* did."

Worf stopped and studied the woman standing beside Crusher. She was older, with streaks of iron in her hair; Romulans were long-lived, like the Vulcans, and this woman had probably lived well over a century. She had probably been alive when the Romulans were still out massacring humans; definitely alive when his parents had been killed at Khitomer. For a moment, he thought of asking her what she thought of such deeds, whether she had approved of them when they had happened.

Then he considered: Whatever this doctor had thought, whatever she might have done herself, she was here now, aboard the *Enterprise,* helping as best she could. She was working to save lives, not take them.

Worf looked at Dr. Venora and forced himself not to see the ruins of Khitomer, not to imagine his parents' death-cries. Instead, he saw a tall, slender woman with dark hair; a woman who smiled at him.

"Thank you," he told the Romulan. "Thank you for saving my life."

Hours later, in the captain's quarters, a quiet group had gathered: Beverly, Worf, and Geordi, now dressed in their regular uniforms. Picard had called them there, and upon their arrival, had served each a glass of the precious Chateau Picard wine. They spoke little, but settled comfortably in the cabin—

exhausted, Picard knew, by the events that had very nearly taken each of their lives, and had claimed the life of their dear friend.

Per instructions, Riker and Deanna entered without sounding the door chime; Picard was ready for them, and handed each a glass of wine. The look Will gave him, and then Deanna, was most difficult for the captain to bear. Riker leaned against the desk, his arm around Deanna.

A moment of silence followed; then Picard regarded them each, one by one, and slowly raised his glass.

"To absent friends," he said evenly. "To family."

As they had so recently at Will and Deanna's wedding, they lifted their glasses, then drank; but this time, there was no joy in the gesture. It seemed wrong to be so grim, Picard decided, when everything about Data's existence had been so joyous.

As if sensing this, Deanna leaned against Will and gazed up at him; and Will, bless him, understood, and smiled as only he could smile. When he spoke, his tone was light, as it should be for a celebration.

"The first time I met Data," he said, "he was standing against a tree in the holodeck, whistling. I thought he was the funniest thing I'd ever seen."

Riker's mood was as contagious as his grin; the others smiled at once, if at first a bit wanly. Picard was surprised to feel his own lips curving upward; he had not thought to find himself smiling again so soon.

"No matter what he did," Riker continued, "he just couldn't get that damn tune right."

Geordi chimed in with sudden enthusiasm. "And he couldn't tell a joke to save his life . . ." At this, Deanna and Beverly laughed aloud. "Do you remember when he created that holodeck program so he could practice stand-up comedy. . . ?"

Picard listened to them all, smiled at them all, as they remembered the happiest times of Data's life, of their own lives where his had touched theirs. And as he did, he promised himself and Data most solemnly to accept Data's sacrifice with joy, not guilt; to let the fact that Data had given his life for Picard's to make Picard's remaining years more precious, more meaningful, knowing they had been bought at such a price . . .

The hardest thing, for Geordi La Forge, was not the terrible shock of realizing his friend was dead, or of speaking about him during the wake, but in returning to Data's cabin and packing up his belongings. It might have been easier had Geordi gone alone, without Worf, who had insisted on coming; at least then, Geordi could allow himself the release of tears without horrifying the Klingon. For Worf's sake, Geordi held them back.

But Data's presence was palpable everywhere: One would never have known, from entering the android's quarters, that the inhabitant was not human. Signs of individuality, even eccentricity, were everywhere. The Sherlock Holmes deerstalker's hat. The violin. Data's paintings.

Geordi picked up the curved Holmes pipe from the dresser and held its bowl in his hand, studying it deeply. He had never felt closer to Data; yet Data had never been farther away.

He glanced up at the sound of something on the dresser being knocked over. A distinct *meow* followed, then Data's orange tabby, Spot, jumped onto a console and looked pointedly up at the two officers.

Geordi glanced at Worf, who returned a helpless look. What, indeed, should be done with the cat? Data would probably want Geordi to care for it, since the engineer was his closest friend, and Geordi prepared himself to take the cat, search for its toys and bowls . . .

But Spot made his own decision. Without hesitation, the cat leaped into Worf's arms. The startled Klingon held the animal with an uncomfortable expression.

"I am not," Worf insisted in his bass voice, "a 'cat person.' "

"I think you are now," Geordi said.

Worf looked down at the cat, who nestled comfortably into the Klingon's strong arms and began purring happily. Worf let go an exasperated, if suspiciously tender, sigh as Geordi grinned at the pair.

That same night, sleep had eluded Picard. The realization came to him that he *had* to speak to someone—someone in particular, and unburden his heart about the amazing being that Data had been, about all that Data had meant to him, had taught him. His grief allowed him no option.

And so he had gone very late down the darkened corridors, and brought that someone back to his quarters. He had sat down at his desk and told the entire story of Data, from the first time he met the android, until the moment of Data's heroic sacrifice, which saved them all.

As Picard at last finished, he said, "I don't know if all this has made sense to you, but I wanted you to know what kind of man he was." He used the term quite intentionally; if anyone had ever earned the term, Data had. "In his quest to be more like us, he helped show us what it means to be human."

Across from him sat the B-4. He wore Data's features, Data's body, but the blankness of his expression tore at Picard's heart. Still, there was a hint of effort there, of an attempt to understand. "My brother was not human," the B-4 said.

"No, he wasn't," Picard replied. "But his wonder and his curiosity about every facet of human life helped all of us see the best parts of ourselves. He embraced change because he always wanted to be more than he was."

"I do not understand."

Picard sighed heavily. "Well, I hope someday you will."

Worf's voice interrupted on comm. "Captain, the *Hemingway* has arrived to tow us to spacedock."

Picard straightened. "On my way. Please notify Commander Riker . . ." He stood, then glanced down at the B-4. "We'll talk later?"

The B-4 failed to respond; he was staring blankly at the bulkhead. Picard squelched a fresh surge of grief at the sight; it was foolish of him to have thought that he could make the B-4 understand what his "brother" had been. And it was enormously difficult, looking at a face that was Data's, when Data's intelligence, Data's curiosity, were so obviously absent.

Picard moved from behind the desk and headed from the door.

Behind him, the B-4 murmured something.

"Never saw the sun . . ."

Picard turned back at once. He had been mistaken; it had not been blankness in the B-4's eyes as the android stared at the wall. The creature was struggling; struggling to remember something important.

"Never saw the sun," the B-4 repeated, this time more firmly.

"Shining so bright," Picard prompted, his voice a near whisper.

"Shining so bright," the android echoed. "Never saw things . . . Never saw things . . ."

"Going so right," Picard recited.

"Going so right." And the android fell silent, as if recitation of the single verse had somehow satisfied it for the time.

Picard waited, the skin on his arms pricking; for an instant, he was near weeping. But the B-4 did not speak again; and at last, Picard gathered himself and left.

Within weeks, the *Enterprise* was in spacedock over Earth, enclosed in a great womb of scaffolding whence she would be reborn, ready once more for space. Picard himself was feeling younger; though by rights the battle with Shinzon and grief over Data's death should have aged him, he had promised himself for the android's sake to approach life with renewed zeal.

Thus it was with great pleasure that he sat in his ready room, the light reflecting beautifully off the undamaged crystalline starship replica nearby, and smiled at the image of Beverly Crusher on his viewscreen.

She sat in her spanking new office at Starfleet Medical, complaining loudly and clearly enjoying herself immensely. She, too, seemed invigorated by the changes in her life. "You can't imagine them, Jean-Luc. They're kids! All with advanced degrees in xenobiology and out to conquer every disease in the quadrant."

Picard's grin widened. "Reminds me of a young doctor I used to know . . ."

"They're running me ragged. Nothing but questions day

and night . . . I love it! Come to dinner and I'll tell you all about it. There's a Bajoran band at the officers' mess."

"I'd love to," Picard said quite honestly, "but I have so much work here."

She understood, and gave him a small, tender smile. "Soon then . . . I'll save the last dance for you."

Her image faded; then the screen darkened. Picard looked up as the door chime sounded. "Come."

Will Riker entered, looking significantly more suntanned than he had a few weeks before. Picard did not need to ask him how he had found things on the Opal Sea.

Weeks earlier, before Will and Deanna had departed for their honeymoon, Picard had taken his leave of Counselor Troi. The counselor had appeared in civilian clothing, her long dark hair falling straight upon her shoulders, framing a face that made no effort to hide her emotions.

"I'm sensing a great deal of sadness," she told Picard, with a half hearted attempt of humor; life with Will had definitely rubbed off on her. "And it's coming from me. I'll miss you, Captain."

She hugged Picard; he returned the gesture wholeheartedly, then pulled back to look at her with a determined smile. "And I'm sensing optimism for the future. We are both going to where we need to be, where we'll be happiest."

Deanna forced a smile and in a lighter tone said, "The Opal Sea."

"And while you're there, Counselor," Picard said, effecting his best sternly paternal manner, "do me a favor . . ."

She waited, expectant.

"*Don't* think of me. Consider that an order."

She had gleefully agreed; and on that note, they had parted. Now the time had come to say farewell to her husband.

"Will," the captain said heartily, and was surprised to find that his throat had tightened.

Riker stood at attention. He was tense, Picard saw, at the realization that this was, in fact, good-bye. "Permission to disembark, sir."

Picard stood and smiled, despite the sudden overwhelming realization of all to whom he was saying farewell: Data. Beverly. Deanna. Will. "Granted," the captain said, with forced ease. "Where's the *Titan* off to?"

It was Riker's turn to smile. "The Neutral Zone . . . We'll be heading up the new task force. Apparently the Romulans are interested in talking."

Picard let himself be proud. "I couldn't think of a better man for the job." He paused, and when he spoke again, his tone was gravely serious. "If I could offer you one piece of advice about your first command?"

"Anything." Riker was as solemn and sincere as the captain had ever seen him.

"When your first officer insists that you can't go on away missions . . ." Picard began lightly.

Will finished with him. "Ignore him."

Riker grinned as the two of them finished the chorus. "I intend to." And then his grin faded, and his manner once again became solemn—so solemn that he added, with clear difficulty: "Serving with you has been an honor."

Picard gazed on him with frank affection and admiration. "The honor was mine . . . Captain Riker." He offered his hand; Riker gripped it, then turned and was gone.

• • •

Riker stepped from the captain's ready room into chaos on the bridge; he had to dodge two technicians working nearby beneath a console. At the engineering station, Geordi was working with a young officer, while Worf stood, arms crossed, scowling at a young ensign who was busy installing Picard's new command chair.

Riker glanced up: a force field still shimmered in place at the gaping wound in the bridge hull, and the sight tugged at him, making him think of Data. It was hard, leaving the *Enterprise* and all the memories aboard her; and, as was Riker's wont, he tried to think of some way to lighten his mood.

It was at that instant that a fresh-faced young officer— Caucasian-looking, with dark hair, probably of full Earth blood—approached him.

"Captain Riker?" the younger man asked, his tone tentative. "Martin Madden, I'm the new first officer."

Riker regarded him. Intelligent, nervous, and far too overeager. "Commander," he said politely.

"I haven't, um, met the captain yet." Madden caught himself fidgeting and made himself stop at once. "I was hoping you could give me a little insight."

"Oh," Riker said . . . then smiled. "Well, the most important thing you need to know is that Captain Picard's not one of those by-the-book officers. He likes to keep things casual. In fact, if you really want to get on his good side . . . call him 'Jean-Luc.' "

Madden returned Riker's smile brightly. "Thank you, sir."

Riker nodded, satisfied with himself, and moved toward the turbolift; on the way, he suddenly stopped and turned.

He took one last look at the *Enterprise,* his home for the last fifteen years: the bridge with her recent battle scars still showing, but with repairs underway. Changing, as she had always changed, yet always remaining the same.

Worf and Geordi both saw, both shared looks and smiles with him.

Then Captain William Riker drew in a deep breath, turned and entered the turbolift, and was gone.

Picard emerged onto the bridge from his ready room, a few padds in one hand. The activity on the bridge suited him after the long period of inactivity as the *Enterprise* was towed home. He was most curious about what was going on at his command chair—but before he could near it, he was approached by a young officer whose face looked extremely familiar. He remembered it from the young man's dossier just as the officer announced:

"Commander Martin Madden reporting for duty, sir."

Picard shook his hand; Madden's was cool, slightly sweaty. "Welcome aboard, Commander," he said, his tone relaxed in hopes of putting the young man at ease. "I hope your transfer didn't come as too much of a surprise."

"I was . . . honored," Madden said.

Picard gave a nod, accepting the compliment. "I needed you immediately to oversee the refit . . ." He inclined his head at the chaos surrounding them. "As you can see, we have a lot to discuss. Shall we say dinner in my quarters at nineteen hundred hours?"

"Very good . . ." Madden hesitated, then added with knowing casualness, "Jean-Luc."

Picard scowled slightly and studied Madden the way a hawk studies its prey shortly before diving for it.

The young man blanched. "Captain Riker was pulling my leg, wasn't he?"

Picard answered only with The Look. He left Madden slightly dazed and aghast, and went over to his chair, where Worf was clearly at odds with the young ensign who was installing it.

"We should wait until the captain—" Worf began, then broke off at the sight of Picard. "Sir."

The ensign kneeling at the side of the chair said confidently, "It's the mark seven, Captain. State-of-the-art ergonomics . . . command interfaces with—"

"I told him you're comfortable with your old chair," Worf interrupted.

"Let's give it a try," Picard said. He settled into it with relish, and looked around him at the repairs to the bridge, at the fresh-faced kids who had joined his crew. They, too, would learn and gain experience, and he would learn with them, even as he taught.

And then he realized Worf and the ensign were waiting expectantly for his judgment on the new chair.

"Feels good," Picard announced, much to the Klingon's disgust and the ensign's pleasure. He did not miss the look of surprise Worf and Geordi shared.

Eagerly, the ensign pointed to a control. "Try that button, sir."

Picard pressed it. Immediately, metal restraints flew into position around his waist and shoulders. The captain was startled at first; then he smiled. "It's about time." He pressed the control again, and the restraints retracted at once.

Delighted, Picard turned to his new first officer. "Commander, please sit down . . ."

Madden sat in Will Riker's old chair; Picard leaned forward to share a padd with him.

"We've received our first assignment," the captain said, with a sudden sense of peace. All was well; he was working, doing what he loved, and grateful to Data for the ability to be exactly where he, Picard, was at the moment—on the *Enterprise* bridge. "We're going to be exploring the Denab system. It should be exciting. It's a place . . . where no one has gone before."

What he did not know was that, in Data's old quarters, the B-4 was remembering, and singing . . .

Never saw the sun
Shining so bright,
Never saw things
Going so right.
Noticing the days
Hurrying by-
When you're in love,
My how they fly!

Nothing but bluebirds
All day long.

A First Look at

STAR TREK NEMESIS

A First Look at

STAR TREK NEMESIS

Michael Klastorin
Production Publicist
for the Motion Picture

A note to the reader: I was lucky enough to be offered the position of unit publicist for the upcoming Star Trek *movie. As the publicist—the person who would release information to the press, work with the still photographer and generally chronicle the making of the film—I was on the set every day of production. I am delighted to have the opportunity to share a little of my experience with you. I grew up with* Star Trek *and very much enjoyed* Star Trek: The Next Generation *and the subsequent series. I am a fan. If you haven't read the novelization preceding this section or seen the movie yet, then what are you doing here? Go . . . right out . . . to the theater. Then we can talk. If you have done these aforementioned things . . . read on. I hope it's as interesting to you as it was exciting to me.*

Star Trek Nemesis began principal photography on November 26, 2001, in the Mojave Desert, just miles away from Edwards Air Force Base. The week spent on location was dedicated to shooting the film's one exterior scene, where Picard, Data, and Worf take a shuttle to the desert planet of Kolarus. Once there, they discover the scattered pieces of a prototype android, B-4. Along the way, they have a run-in with the planet's inhabitants, who are not very welcoming to the visitors.

The scene in the desert gave first-time *Star Trek* Director Stuart Baird a chance to establish the pace of the action that was to come. "This scene comes fairly early in the film," says Baird, "and as such, I wanted to invest it with equal amounts of fun and action. Before they are chased by the Kolarans, I had a chance to showcase the seldom seen 'fun' side of Picard."

For Patrick Stewart, the scene worked on all the levels Baird had hoped for, as he found himself in the driver's seat of a twenty-fourth century off-road vehicle. "It was extremely powerful, and I got a lot of pleasure out of driving it," Stewart says. The vehicle was designed by Ivan Stewart, who is recognized as the king of off-road racing, and it performed remarkably. Weeks before the scene was filmed, Stewart was taken to a quarry area to get some practice. When it came time to go in front of the cameras, the actor made full use of his training, and did more than ninety percent of the driving required for the spectacular chase scene.

The stopover on Kolarus would also provide Makeup Super-

The discovery of another Soong android is the catalyst for the feature's storyline.

visor Michael Westmore with the challenge of creating a heretofore-unseen alien species—a task with which he's not unfamiliar. "Since the planet Kolarus is a desert environment, I decided to go with something you would basically find in the desert. On *Star Trek* we'd already been through lizards, crocodiles, and snakes, but this time I found a book about turtles, and the shapes and patterns of their shells. I designed the species with a turtle pattern that goes up the front of their heads. In painting them, I had my technicians actually look at the backs of the turtles to get the patterns of the tortoiseshell just right. We shined them up to get the shell look to it, and made the skin a little broken up as if it's caked with dirt." Westmore also incorporated the turtle look in the eyes and teeth of the characters. In preparation for the actual filming, thirty stuntmen arose at 4:00 AM to get their makeup applied for the arduous days of shooting.

At the conclusion of the scene, the cast and crew made their way back to Los Angeles and Paramount Studios, where the rest of the film would be shot.

In the preproduction stage of the film, many discussions were held about the guests at Troi and Riker's wedding reception. While Rick Berman would have loved to invite a plethora of actors who had appeared during the run of the series, it ultimately came down to scheduling and film time. There was however one very special guest at the wedding who didn't make it in front of he cameras. Filming stopped for over forty-five minutes (a very costly amount in the world of production) as former United States Secretary of State Madeleine Albright dropped by to see her close friend Patrick Stewart. The former secretary, a very big *Star Trek* fan, was in Southern California for a speaking engagement. She posed with the delighted and honored cast for a photo and was presented with the slate (the device used to identify the scene and take number for the editor) by Rick Berman.

Marina Sirtis was adorned in a twenty-fourth century bridal gown designed by Costume Design Consultant Robert Blackman, and both she and Jonathan Frakes decided to wear

A rehearsal for the captain's toast to the newlyweds.

their own wedding rings. Since the scene starts at the reception after the actual ceremony, there were no prewedding jitters to worry about for the actors. "The wedding was a lot of fun for me," Sirtis says, "because whether you're a real bride or a make-believe bride, you're the princess for the day. In our case, it was two days."

"I didn't realize until we were in the middle of shooting that scene," remarks Frakes, "how easy it is to be the person who has gotten married in terms of the amount of work you have to do. Everything is being said *about* you. All I had to do was put on my dress uniform, get my hair sprayed into place, react and enjoy."

The joyous union on-camera served as a joyful reunion off-camera, and gave cast members an eerie sense of déjà vu. For Patrick Stewart it ". . . had a slightly unnerving feeling, in a kind of Rip Van Winkle way. We've been asleep and suddenly woken, and nothing has changed. But the relationships between this whole group of people have simply deepened and strengthened over the years. That's the principal delight in being back the ensemble work that goes on in these movies."

"It's like putting on your favorite old sweater or a hand-made pair of boots that you've had for years and years," LeVar Burton says of returning to his character of Geordi La Forge, "and even better than that is being able come on the soundstage and you have a shorthand and a history, and even though three years have gone by, it's like no time has passed. It's spooky, but in a good way. Every time we do a film, we pick it up as if we were doing this the previous day, as opposed to in this case, three years ago."

"We were filming in the corridors of the *Enterprise*," recalls Frakes, "sitting in our chairs, each of us doing what we do while the crew sets the lighting, and I looked over and there's Patrick and there's Brent and Marina and LeVar, and the same kibitzing took place and the same ease of dialogue, the same total lack of respect that we've all cherished over the years. It was as if time had stopped. As if none of us had done anything but fly the *Enterprise* for the past fifteen years. There was a comfort to it, an ease to it, a pleasure of being back in the company of these friends—these intelligent, talented, funny, complicated friends that we have all become."

"People ask me how excited I am to see my old friends again," says Michael Dorn, "and the honest truth is that I see them all the time. Marina is one of my best friends, and I talk to Patrick, Jonathan, LeVar, Brent, and Gates often. We go out to dinner frequently. It's great to all be working together again, but it's not like I haven't seen these people since the last film."

While Director Stuart Baird could only shake his head and smile (he had little other choice), the cast assumed their "normal" way of working as soon as they arrived on the set, which

Frakes found it very relaxing to let someone else worry about the next shot.

meant laughing, joking and fooling around until the very second that Baird called "Action!" Sometimes that levity extended into the take. Two brief examples:

Picard is briefing his crew before going into battle, telling them the severity of their situation. He finishes a long, solemn speech with some final encouragement for his brave crew. Then he points to Michael Dorn. "And you, Mister Worf," he commands, "there will be no hiding in your room in the closet while we go off to face almost certain death."

As Picard and Data prepare to face off in a phaser fight against dozens of Remans, Stewart and Spiner discuss their inspirations for the moment.

"I'm going to think Bruce Willis," says Stewart.

"And I'm going to think Cybill Shepherd," replies Spiner.

For all the joy and comfort in being reunited with his long-time friends, Frakes adds, "it was also nice to meet some new friends."

Those new friends included actors Tom Hardy and Ron Perlman, who were more than eager to join the ranks of *Star Trek*'s infamous villains. Says Hardy of his character of Shinzon, "John Logan wrote a Greek classic using the characters and surroundings of the *Star Trek* universe. Shinzon is a dynamic, young, bitter helpless individual who comes to battle the man he was supposed to be . . . the man he felt he *deserved* to be. He's a character who is torn between all he knows based on his past, and what he believes he has the potential to be in the form of Picard." It intrigued Hardy that Logan had invested the character with more than just a superficial villain mentality and motivations. "Shinzon, for all intents and purposes, doesn't exist. He has no father, no his-

A land-based vehicle, seemingly out of place in the futuristic terrain of a *Star Trek* feature, provided one of the climactic sequences in the film.

tory. That creates a jealousy and bitterness in him when he meets Picard, but it's tempered by the pure unadulterated excitement of being able to find out about himself. As an actor, to be able to find the human soul within the character makes him so much more of an interesting villain."

The casting of Shinzon proved to be a demanding task for the filmmakers. "We needed to find a young actor who looked enough like Patrick Stewart so that the audience could believe that this was a younger version, a clone of him," *Star Trek* Producer Rick Berman explains. "We literally met with hundreds of actors. We found some who looked like Patrick, who weren't very good actors, and some who were very good actors, and didn't much look like Patrick. Then a tape came from London, and while it was not representative of what Tom was capable of, there was something in it that caught our attention. We got another tape, and then flew him over to read for the studio. Everybody saw something special in his performance. I think Tom has the makings of a very big star."

Patrick Stewart gave Hardy high praise for his technique and performance in handling a very demanding role. "He studied some of our movies and was encouraged to try to absorb the aspects of the way I have portrayed Picard, but his experiences clearly make him sound different, move differently, different attitudes. What was hardest was to get those appearances of physical similarity. It's not easy to find an actor who can inhabit the technical demands of the role, while also having to look like someone else. He came through splendidly."

While Tom Hardy bore some resemblance to Patrick Stewart, there were still some adjustments to be made before he could appear on screen. Michael Westmore recalls, "Tom has a very short nose, while Patrick's is longer. Patrick has a cleft in his chin and Tom doesn't. I already had a cast of Patrick's face, and I took one of Tom's as well. Using those elements, I sculpted a latex nose and chin that Tom could wear in the film. I also took a cast of Patrick's teeth, duplicated them in acrylic, and Tom slipped this very thin little veneer over his teeth right before every scene. We shaved his head, and those few little things are enough that when the two of them do profiles and are in the scenes together, you have the feeling there's a definite relationship there."

In Shinzon, actor Tom Hardy created a villain who was literally the equal of Picard.

Although Hardy went through the process happily, he did feel there was a bit of inequity in the makeup trailer. "Here I am playing a clone of Patrick Stewart, and he comes in, takes about fifteen minutes to get his makeup on, and I sit there for a couple of hours getting the nose and chin glued on." That would prove to be only the beginning.

Having accomplished his first makeover of Hardy, Westmore was not yet done with the actor. During the course of the film, Shinzon suffers from a degenerative disease that rapidly

Although he was covered with layers of makeup and appliances, Ron Perlman's performance as the sinister Reman viceroy is chilling.

ages him as his condition worsens. "As the movie progresses, Shinzon is starting to wither and die. We didn't want to use appliances, but there had to be something to show that he was disintegrating. We established six stages that he would go through. His first appearance in the film in stage one, where he appears relatively healthy. In stage two, we start to see a few blood veins on his face. By stage six, the final stage, his whole head and the back of his hands are covered in blood veins." To achieve the effects of the disease, Westmore physically hand-painted dozens of blue veins on the actor's head and hands. "There wasn't a stencil I could use, so after I established a stage of the disease, we would photograph it all around. I would use the picture as my guide. Tom also came up with the idea to show a little bit more of the process with the use of contact lenses. In stage five, we used a contact lens that started to white out the irises of his eyes. In the final sage, the lenses were even whiter, and we applied red around them."

Hardy wasn't alone during those long hours in the makeup chair. Both Michael Dorn and Brent Spiner went through their individual transformations into Worf and Data, respectively, as they had during their seven seasons on the television show and the three previous feature films. Also joining the men was another cast member who was no stranger to prosthetics.

In his three seasons as the star of the hit television series *Beauty and the Beast,* Ron Perlman had to endure a grueling four hours every day in the makeup trailer. For his transformation to the Reman viceroy, the actor merely had to sit for about two-and-a-half hours.

Although he confesses not to have been a follower of the *Star Trek* series or films, he accepted his role in *Nemesis* gladly. "*Star Trek* is part of the American quilt," says Perlman, "It's iconic. The great thing is that I came to this project in the most objective way possible, and John Logan's script is a world-class piece of writing. I was thrilled with how smart it was. How unpredictable it was. How act-able it was. My character is kind of like the power behind the power, kind of a little bit like Iago. We very rarely get to see him emerge in any kind of revealing way. He's shrouded in mystery, which is what drew me to the character. The particular challenge was to communicate the who and the why in a minimal, selective way, rooted in stillness, where nothing is given away. What you see of the viceroy is like an iceberg. You're only seeing a small fraction of who he really is. That's a cool thing for an actor to wrap his teeth around."

Perlman also had the luxury of playing an alien species that had never been seen by audiences before. "We've never seen the Remans, so it's kind of cool to present something that's fresh and uncharted. A mysterious race."

In his creation of that race, Michael Westmore started with the script. "We're told that the Remans live on a planet that only gets sun a fraction of the time, so they have developed without the benefit of sunshine. They do best in darkness. Stuart Baird and Rick Berman had the idea that they wanted the Remans to have an almost Nosferatulike feeling, but without making them into vampires."

Perlman, who was covered from head to toe between costume and prosthetics, used both to further his creation of the character. "It's a different kind of performance when you're playing an abstraction, which is what the viceroy is. When you play characters that are heavily influenced by the makeup, you have to reserve a great deal of your decisions about the character until you have finally made the full transformation. What you look like is going to affect what you sound like, how you move, and the whole history of how you might have lived your life. In turn that is going to affect who you are, and what's at stake for you in any given situation."

One of Perlman's first scenes to be filmed was the climac-

This very earnest lieutenant is *X-Men* director Bryan Singer.

tic fight between his character and Will Riker. That, too, presented a challenge. "The costume itself goes from the top of my toes to the top of my neck, and it's made out of vinyl, which is totally nonporous. The jacket, which is the crowning achievement of the costume, is made of thick vinyl. Basically, when I'm in it, my skin and pores are not breathing. This is complicated by the fact that my head is totally covered in prosthetic makeup, so there's no breathing anywhere except through my mouth or nostrils. That made for a physical challenge that I hadn't quite prepared myself for. We had six days of shooting on a very elaborately staged fight. It was all I could do to muster the energy when they said 'action' to do what I needed to do. The great thing about it was that Jonathan Frakes is one of my favorite people on the planet.

"We did a play together in Los Angeles about sixteen years ago. We both liked to get to the theater a couple of hours before anyone else, just to relax and get into the mindset of the performance that night. And one day, I walked in and Jonathan was kind of pacing around in front of the theater, and he had a little smirk on his face, and what basically happened was this:

PERLMAN: Well, you look like the cat who
    swallowed the canary.
FRAKES: Well, I've had a really good day.
PERLMAN: That's funny. I've had a really good
    day too.
FRAKES: Well, I bet you haven't had as good a day
    as I've had.
PERLMAN: OK . . . you go first.

FRAKES: I just got the second lead on the new *Star
Trek* series. How about you?

PERLMAN: I just got the Beast on *Beauty and the
Beast*.

"That day changed both of our lives. In the breaks between
shooting on *Nemesis,* we reminisced, caught up with each
other, and basically laughed. The great time I had with him
superceded the physical annoyances of what I had to go
through."

For Rick Berman, and ultimately Stuart Baird, one of the
advantages of *Star Trek* was its long production history. "Over
the course of fifteen years," says Berman, "we've put together
a family of people. Herman Zimmerman, Michael Westmore,
Marty Hornstein, Peter Lauritson, and many others who have
come to know each other intimately. We can communicate in
shorthand and as a result, we don't have that period on a film
where everyone has to get to know each other and adjust to
each other's style of work. That saves a lot of time." Stuart
Baird was able to tap into the knowledge of all the *Star Trek*
veterans, and in some cases, the cast gave him a little extra
help.

"We were doing a scene in the observation lounge of the
Enterprise," recalls Frakes, "Stuart wisely thought that
since this was a gathering of senior officers, that to add an
elegant older gentleman as an officer in the background
would make sense. When the lighting was done and we all
walked onto the set, we saw this distinguished actor in one
of the chairs, and to a person, we explained to Stuart that he
had put a stranger into an intimate circle of friends, who

Director Stuart Baird (left) and Producer Rick Berman on the bridge set.

doesn't say anything, hasn't been seen before, and whose presence would be questioned immediately by the audience." The director took the advice of his cast and removed the actor from the scene.

Herman Zimmerman, who began his *Star Trek* career working with Gene Roddenberry in the creation of *The Next Generation* series, went on to *Star Trek: Deep Space Nine* and

Enterprise. He also worked on the previous five *Star Trek* feature films. With all that experience, Zimmerman still finds his work a happy challenge. "For this film we've created about thirty different environments," says the production designer. "The ideas came out of John Logan's script, his writing raised the bar in the level of scope and design. The *Scimitar,* Shinzon's ship, is described as being about three times as large as the *Enterprise,* which is the largest starship the Federation has ever made. So this is a big, nasty machine. It also carries a devastating weapon, which can destroy planets. That in itself was a good design challenge."

For the design of the *Scimitar,* Zimmerman began with the

Seen from a catwalk high above the soundstage: the floor of the Romulan Senate.

history of the Remans, courtesy of the imaginations of John Logan, Rick Berman, and Brent Spiner. "The Remans live in the dark and have very weak eyes, and their planet, Remus, is basically a dilithium mining community. This inspired me to design their ship with a dark, metallic quality. I also took a design cue from a breastplate that the wardrobe designer had made for the Remans. I extrapolated that into the kind of cross bracing you might need if you were building a very large spaceship. It's a design motif that carries through everything. It eventually got back to the wardrobe department in the form of belt buckles that were designed for the uniforms. It became kind of a round robin thing."

The fully realized Romulan Senate, as seen in the film.

Zimmerman's sets did indeed reflect the enormity that was intended in their original conception. While the bridge of the *Enterprise* occupies only a third of a soundstage, the bridge of the *Scimitar* took up almost the entire structure, as did the sets for the corridors and observation lounge of the enemy vessel, as well as the Romulan Senate and the Alaska pavilion for Riker and Troi's reception.

For all concerned, Zimmerman's designs went far beyond what anyone had expected. "There's nothing greater than walking on a set," Perlman explains, "and having it fill you with a certain kind of power just because of its magnitude and scope and sophistication and beauty. I have not worked on one set on this movie that was anything short of that." Tom Hardy was equally enamored of the final results. "Just standing on the bridge of the *Enterprise* was impressive enough to make me realize what an amazing world I was now part of, but when I saw the bridge of my ship, it took my breath away. I couldn't believe this was all mine. I can't even drive. I don't have a license. But this is my ride."

Although the *Enterprise* is basically the same ship that was seen in the two previous features, Zimmerman was still able to tinker with the ship without greatly altering its long-standing character. "I chose a few more metallic colors, which, in collaboration with Jeffrey Kimball's amazing cinematography, will enrich the colors on the screen."

The biggest alteration of the *Enterprise* was not in the ship, but *under* it, courtesy of Terry Frazee, the film's special effects coordinator. In the past, when the *Enterprise* engaged in battle, for the most part, the hits taken by the ship were realized by the actors moving while the camera was shaken. In

Nemesis, the *Enterprise* is pitted against her most ferocious adversary and the ship is truly tested to its limits. To add an even greater degree of realism to the battle scenes, Frazee constructed a metal framework underneath the bridge set. Twenty airbags were mounted in the framework and inflated by a compressor. Each airbag was designed to lift 14,000 pounds, and when fully inflated, lifted the bridge about twelve inches off its normal base. At the touch of a button, signaled by Baird, the bags deflated instantly, giving both the set and the actors in it a realistic jolt that required no acting. Frazee was able to move the set in any direction that the action called for, so that Baird could film the *Enterprise* crew in their most intense battle ever put on the screen. (For this writer, the sensation was akin to being on the Las Vegas attraction—*Star Trek: The Experience,* a lot of jolts and shakes, but *I've* got the whole cast right here with me.)

Principal photography on *Star Trek Nemesis* was completed on March 7, 2002. As the production wrapped, Rick Berman was more than satisfied that Stuart Baird had given the film exactly what he had hoped for. "I've seen probably a quarter of the film cut together at this point, and all the rushes, and Stuart has made an extraordinary movie. He's given it a scope and grandeur that we've never had in the previous films."

Baird was also satisfied that the arduous journey he had undertaken was well worth the trip. "Everyone was very generous in sharing their vast experience. I think they were also somewhat energized by having a director who didn't come with a Ph.D. in *Star Trek.* Rick was tremendously supportive with his knowledge, his experience, and very generous with his encouragement. After all is said and done, I hope this movie is one that can both be appreciated by the fans, and give those who have never been to a *Star Trek* movie an exciting ride and a great introduction to a wonderful new galaxy."

For screenwriter and ardent *Star Trek* fan John Logan, the project exceeded his wildest imagination. "It's a very rare occurrence for a screenwriter to actually see a film on the screen that looks the way he hoped it would. The movie that I imagined in my head came to life. When we started this, Brent Spiner told me that by the end of the process, I was

Brent Spiner and John Logan, two of the writers responsible for *Nemesis*'s story, chat between takes.

going to be sick of *Star Trek*. He couldn't have been more wrong. If it's possible, my admiration has only grown through the process."

As for the cast, after one hundred seventy-nine episodes of the series, and now, four feature films, they remain as loyal and as fond of their characters as they are of each other. Will there be a *Star Trek XI*? Is *Nemesis* the last appearance of *The Next Generation* crew?

Jonathan Frakes has his own idea about the future. "Now that they, in their infinite wisdom have married off Deanna Troi to Captain Riker, we are in fertile territory for the half hour sitcom—*The Rikers*. Their wacky Uncle Data and their dog Worf. I'm not sure that we can afford them, but certainly the Rikers in space. I think there's something there. A cross between *The Jetsons, Bewitched,* and *Married With Children*. I'm thinking a half hour." On a more serious note, when asked if he would return to play Riker in a future *Star Trek* film, the actor responds instantly—"In a heartbeat. This is the role that changed my life in all sorts of ways. I'd do it gladly. Gladly and fondly."

Frakes's sentiment is echoed by the entire cast.

"I always look forward to being Picard and to being with this ensemble of actors, whether it's professionally or socially," says Patrick Stewart, "and I don't feel that any of us are done with our characters. If this *is* the last movie, I am very much at peace with the kind of movie that it is, and certainly after fifteen years, with a lot of bright prospects ahead of me, I would feel fine to call this closure. But I believe that there is the potential for a great sequel to the *Nemesis* story."

And what does Rick Berman foresee for the *Star Trek* fea-

ture film franchise? Now that Riker, Troi, and Dr. Crusher have left the ship, and Data is gone, is there room for Seven of Nine or Julian Bashir on the *Enterprise*-E? Is Data really gone? Will we see the crew together again on screen?

"This is *Star Trek*," smiles the producer. "Anything is possible."